The
Army Doctor's
Baby

Helen Scott Taylor

Other Books in the Army Doctor's Series

Acknowledgments

Thanks go to my wonderful critique partner Mona Risk who is always there when I need her help, to my son Peter Taylor for creating a gorgeous book cover, and, as always, to my reliable editor Pam Berehulke.

Chapter One

Major Radley Knight opened his parents' front door and stepped into the peaceful sanctuary of Willow House. The familiar surroundings wrapped around him like a hug—the slightly frayed rug, the family photos on the wall, the wide staircase where he'd played as a boy. He dropped his bag, closed his eyes, and breathed in the familiar old-house smell. What a blessed relief to be home.

There had been many days in the last nine months when he'd dreamed of this quiet spot in the English countryside, of the peace and the safety he'd taken for granted. Endless days when his hands had been covered in blood and his head pounding from lack of sleep. Endless days when he feared every loud noise would herald a new group of casualties to the field hospital in Afghanistan where he'd been stationed.

That all seemed like another world now he was home, the only sounds here the rhythmic tick of the grandfather clock on the landing halfway up the stairs, and the clattering of his mother in the kitchen at the end of the hall.

Radley drew in a deep breath and released it slowly. At last he could chill out with no nasty surprises.

A mewling cry broke the silence. What the heck was that? An animal...no, he'd heard a similar sound before,

1

but never in this house.

It was a baby.

Was his mother babysitting? He narrowed his eyes in thought, trying to guess whose baby it might be.

The cry sounded again, louder this time. A definite note of desperation in the high-pitched wail, as though the tiny infant were about to expire from hunger and needed sustenance stat. It compelled his feet to move towards the sound. He pushed open the sitting room door and glanced around.

A woman relaxed in the leather lounger by the French windows, a tiny bundle in her arms. Early morning sun slanted in, gleaming off her long dark hair, turning the smooth skin of her bare breast above the baby's head pale, almost translucent.

The woman's head came up. Her blue eyes fixed on him, wide and inquiring. He stood transfixed by the sight of mother and child, a scene of such natural beauty it seemed surreal after the horrific things he'd witnessed recently.

She was stunning with luxuriant thick hair and brilliant sapphire eyes. He'd never seen her before. He would definitely have remembered. So, what was she doing in his parents' house?

"You must be Radley," she said, her voice pitched low so as not to disturb her baby.

"Yes," he muttered. She knew who he was. Why did he know nothing about her?

His mother's footsteps sounded on the wooden floor behind him. "Radley, darling, you're back. How wonderful. I didn't expect you until later."

He had to consciously drag his gaze away from the woman to look at his mother. "I jumped on a train as soon as we landed at Brize Norton. I just wanted to get home."

His gaze returned to the woman, drawn against his will.

"Come and give me a hug," his mother said. "Don't stand there gawping at Olivia while she feeds George. Allow the poor girl some privacy."

His mother closed the door and threw her arms around his neck. "It's so good to have you back safe and sound."

Radley blinked, trying to gather his thoughts. Being a doctor in the army, he was used to working long hours with little rest. It went with the job. But he must be sleepier than he'd thought because he felt dazed.

"Hello, Mum. It's good to see you." He kissed his mother as she ran an affectionate hand over his stubbly cheek. "That's more like it. You looked as though you were in a trance just now. Come on, I'll make you some breakfast and you can tell me what you've been doing."

He followed his mother down the wood-paneled hall to the back of the house and settled on one of the chairs at the kitchen table. She cracked eggs into a pan and laid strips of bacon on the grill.

"Who is Olivia? I don't remember you mentioning her before."

"Yes, well, that was on purpose. I didn't want you to tell your brother."

"Why? What's she got to do with Cameron?"

His mother gave him a meaningful look over the top of her glasses and things started falling into place. *Olivia...* Now he thought about it, Cameron had mentioned a girl with that name. She'd been his girlfriend in college. There had been some kind of falling-out when he split up with her. Cameron had e-mailed Radley for advice.

"That's not the girl who claimed she was pregnant with Cam's baby?"

"She didn't *claim* to be pregnant; she *was* pregnant." His mother raised her eyebrows. "You've just seen the evidence for yourself."

The woman had obviously wormed her way into his

3

mother's affections. Irritation raced along Radley's nerves. His mother was too softhearted for her own good. Olivia had probably realized Cameron's family had money and turned up on the doorstep with some sob story. He couldn't believe his father had been so easily suckered, though.

"For God's sake, Mum, just because she says Cam is the baby's father doesn't mean it's true. Have you had a DNA test done?"

His mother slammed a pan down on the kitchen counter with a bang that made him jump. "Don't you take *that* attitude, Radley Knight. I'm very unhappy with your brother for the way he's treated Olivia. I don't want you making matters worse. Just because your wife—"

"Ex-wife," he snapped.

"Just because your ex-wife did that to you, doesn't mean all women lie about who fathered their children. Olivia is a decent, honest girl."

Radley pressed his lips together to hold back his retort. Cameron had been certain he couldn't have made his girlfriend pregnant. He would take his brother's word over that of a woman any day, especially one who was obviously taking advantage of his mother's generous nature.

"What did she do, turn up at the door with a baby in her arms and beg you to take her in?"

"No, she did not!"

His mother dropped his plate of breakfast in front of him with a clatter. She frowned and Radley dug into his food, avoiding her glare.

"That wife of yours has a lot to answer for. You used to be kind and generous before she got her claws into you."

"Ex-wife," Radley said under his breath.

"Olivia called from the hospital, trying to contact Cameron. Of course I asked her why. When she told me, I went in to visit. It took me all of thirty seconds to realize she was honest and desperately in need of help. I suggest you eat up then go and get some sleep. Maybe when you're rested you'll be in a better mood and we can have a sensible discussion about this."

In the distance the plaintive cry of the tiny infant started again.

Radley found he'd lost his appetite.

Olivia cuddled her baby and rubbed his back, burping him gently. She pressed her nose to his soft dark hair and inhaled the heavenly baby smell. How she loved this little man. A love so strong it almost hurt. From the moment they'd placed the newborn boy in her arms a week ago, she'd been smitten.

She closed her eyes and whispered against his hair. "I promise I'm going to look after you well, sweetie. We'll be fine together, just the two of us. I'll pass my law exams and get a good job. Then I'll find us a nice place to live."

Cameron Knight had really let her down. When they'd dated in college, she'd known he was an army cadet—that as soon as he passed his medical exams, he'd be off to some war zone to patch up wounded soldiers. She'd never planned to have Cameron's baby and she didn't expect him to marry her, but planned or not, George had come into this world. He was as much Cameron's son as hers. She had expected him to accept that responsibility. Yet the coward hadn't answered a single one of her many texts, e-mails, and calls. He might as well have fallen off the planet.

Anger clenched inside Olivia's chest. She took a deep breath and let it out slowly. If not for Cameron's parents, she didn't know how she would have managed. A soft knock sounded and Sandra Knight put her head around the door.

"Have you finished feeding, love?"

"Yes." Olivia cupped George's head in her palm and glanced down at his face. "He's out for the count now."

"I expect you're ready for this, then." Sandra held up a ceramic mug and the fragrance of coffee filled the room.

"Wonderful. You're a mind reader."

Sandra came in and placed the cup on a small table beside the chair. Cameron's mum was so easy to be around, so normal and down-to-earth. In her jeans and pink sweatshirt she could be any housewife. Nobody would guess she was a doctor. At least while Olivia stayed with the Knights, she didn't need to worry if George fell ill. Both Cameron's parents were doctors. Now Radley had arrived, that meant she potentially had three doctors to help.

Olivia tried to sit up straighter so she could put George in his bassinet to sleep. Pain shot up her body from the C-section wound and she winced.

"Stay still. You shouldn't be lifting him yet. Let me take him for you." Sandra grasped George with the confidence of one well used to handling infants and settled him in his bed. "Shall we check to see how you're healing?"

Olivia eased down the loose waist of her sweatpants. With a swift move, Sandra peeled back the dressing and examined the long, stitched wound across her belly.

"Does it look okay? It still hurts a lot." Olivia stared down at her mottled purple and yellow belly.

"I'm afraid there's a lot of bruising because it was an emergency procedure. Did your obstetrician explain that they did a T-cut in your uterus to get George out quickly?"

"Possibly. Those first few days after the birth, I was so focused on George I didn't really take in everything the doctor said."

"I didn't know until your notes came through to me

yesterday. That's part of the reason you're so sore and why you must take extra care not to lift anything. For your next pregnancy, I expect they'll recommend you have an elective C-section ahead of the due date so they don't risk you going into labor."

Olivia closed her eyes and tried to get her head around the concept of another baby. She was having enough trouble dealing with the reality of one. Sandra must have noticed because she squeezed Olivia's arm. "Don't worry about the future now. Let's just concentrate on getting you healed and back to normal."

While Olivia sipped her coffee, Sandra perched on another chair and folded her hands in her lap. "I'm sorry Radley barged in on you earlier. He's normally more of a gentleman than that."

"No problem. He didn't know I was here." It had given Olivia a shock when she looked up to see him in the doorway. For a moment she'd thought it was Cameron. She'd seen photos of Radley but hadn't realized how alike the two brothers were. They were both tall and dark like their father.

"You'll soon get used to Rad. He's well house-trained and can be quite helpful when he wants to be." Sandra smiled, obviously pleased to have her son home safe and sound. "Anyway," she stood and straightened her glasses, "I'd better let you rest. I always recommend that new mums sleep when their babies do."

"I wish I could. Unfortunately, I need to study."

"There's plenty of time for that. Give yourself a few weeks to heal before you worry about your exams."

Olivia nodded and smiled, but as soon as Sandra left the room, she reached down to retrieve her law textbook from the floor. She placed it on a pillow to protect her sore tummy from the edges of the heavy book.

She turned to the chapter on contract law and sucked in a breath. Feeling ill and then spending weeks in the hospital before the birth had put her so far behind she was almost overwhelmed with the work she had to catch up on, but she had to do it. The college had agreed to let her take her final exams late. They'd given her a second chance; she wouldn't waste it.

Unfortunately, the delay had cost her the internship with a prestigious law firm. She needed to start looking for another firm to take her on in the New Year, after her exam results came through.

It wasn't only her future that hung in the balance, but George's as well. Cameron's parents had been wonderful. They would always help with babysitting, yet she couldn't impose on their hospitality forever.

Radley woke to the sound of a crying baby. He rubbed his eyes and checked the clock. Three p.m., that meant he'd slept for five hours since he arrived home. He threw back the bedcovers and pulled on jeans and a T-shirt. The noise sounded as though it was coming from the room next to his—Cameron's bedroom.

He wandered along the hall and halted at the open door to his brother's bedroom. A nasty smell filled the air. His mother stood by what looked like a baby-changing unit with shelves laden with diapers, creams, and other baby paraphernalia. If he remembered rightly, a chest of drawers had been there before, with Cameron's sporting trophies on top.

"What are you doing, Mum?"

"What does it look like I'm doing?"

She pulled a wet wipe out of a box and cleaned up the bottom end of the tiny baby laid on the plastic changing mat.

"Changing a diaper."

"Well done. You obviously did learn something during your five years at medical school."

"Give me a break. I've only just woken up."

His mother cast him a smile and he realized she'd

been teasing him. Maybe he was still a little prickly after the long journey home from Afghanistan.

He ambled closer to the baby unit and picked up a blue and pink rattle. "What's his name?"

"George, after your father."

Using his father's name... Sounded like Olivia was trying to curry favor with his parents any way she could. He pushed aside the cynical thought and held the rattle a few inches above the baby's face. "Hey, George, what's this?" He gave it a shake. The child stilled its wriggling and seemed to be listening. The kid was cute, like a doll, with his tuft of dark hair and tiny pink-bow mouth.

Radley's mother finished putting on the diaper and buttoned up the blue all-in-one pajama suit the kid was wearing. "There you go, little man, a lovely clean, dry bottom. I bet you feel better for that, don't you, darling." She lifted the baby and kissed his forehead before cuddling him close. "You are such a gorgeous little thing. I could hug you all day. But I've got to go to work. Uncle Radley will take you to your mummy."

Radley retreated. He had no intention of doing anything of the sort. His mother wasn't easily put off, though. She pursued him until his back hit the wall. "No, Mum."

"Yes, Radley. Come on. Make yourself useful."

"I don't know a thing about babies."

"That's nonsense. You're a doctor."

"I'm a trauma specialist."

She dismissed his objection with a roll of her eyes and passed him the baby. With a sigh of resignation, he took the tiny boy into his arms. He was so small and fragile; Radley was afraid he might squeeze him too hard. He adjusted his grip, one hand cupping the baby's padded bottom, the other his back, with the child's head against his shoulder.

Feelings he had pushed down and tried to forget

flooded back on a rush of pain—the night he'd watched his wife give birth to what he'd thought was his son. The first and only time he'd held the baby boy, marveling at this new tiny person in his life. A few hours later another man had turned up and claimed to be the baby's father, and Radley's life had fallen apart. That had been five years ago. He'd thought that episode was behind him. Now he realized he'd been fooling himself.

"What's the matter, Rad?" His mother laid a hand on his shoulder. He hadn't confided in her how bad he felt about losing the son it turned out he'd never had. He wasn't about to open the subject up for discussion now.

"Nothing. Still a bit tired, I guess."

"Okay." She examined his face for a moment longer, then turned and headed off. "I'm sorry to leave you to cope, but I must go or I'll be late. I do two evening surgeries a week at the local practice so their female doctor gets a break."

Halting at the door, she put a hand to her forehead. "I almost forgot to tell you, Olivia had an emergency C-section that involved a T-cut to the womb. She mustn't lift anything, and that includes George. She'll want to feed the little guy soon, so make sure you're around to help out. His stroller is in the back porch. I told Olivia to take a walk in the garden to reduce the risk of blood clots. She's probably still outside. See you later." She raised a hand and was gone.

Radley stood in the quiet room, the baby in his arms, listening to his mother's footsteps descending the stairs. He heard her shout good-bye, then the front door slammed.

George wriggled against him. How vulnerable and defenseless this tiny person was. The urge to protect the baby flooded through Radley, unlocking emotions he'd shut deep inside. He kissed the soft, fluffy hair on

George's head. If Olivia was telling the truth, this was his nephew. It wasn't the same as having his own son, but Knight blood ran through the little boy's veins and right now the child needed him.

A smile pulled at his lips. "You're a funny little guy, aren't you?" He shifted his grip, moving George into a more comfortable position.

He walked to the wall mirror and looked at the reflection of the newborn in his arms. George did look a bit like the baby photos of Cameron. Perhaps he should have advised Cameron to contact Olivia all those months ago when she first claimed to be pregnant, but Cameron had been so certain he wasn't the father. Radley now hoped Cameron was wrong.

Chapter Two

A pair of ducks squabbled on the pond, quacking and splashing. Olivia smiled at their antics and drew in a breath of the clean air. Willow House where the Knights lived was a wonderful country retreat away from the dirt and bustle of London, a fantastic place for kids.

The remains of a tree house balanced on the branches of a massive oak tree at the bottom of the garden. It was neglected now, but in the past she could imagine how much fun Radley and Cameron must have had there. She hoped her little boy would get to enjoy this garden as well when they visited. She still hoped Cameron might change his attitude and play a part in George's life, otherwise it would be difficult for her to maintain a relationship with Cameron's parents. And she wanted to keep that. Not just for George, but for herself as well.

"Hi there."

Olivia started in surprise at the sound of a man's voice. She'd been waiting for Sandra to call her inside to feed George. She turned on the wooden bench where she'd sat to watch the ducks.

Radley strode towards her, George snug against his chest. Olivia's breath caught and her heart gave a jolt. When Radley had appeared at the lounge door earlier, she'd not thought much about him except that he resembled Cameron. But, gosh, the man was good-looking, or maybe it was just the sight of him with her baby in his arms that had her melting inside.

Faded jeans hung low on his hips, and a plain white T-shirt clung to his torso. His biceps bulged, and his forearms were corded with muscle beneath a dusting of dark hair. George looked so tiny cradled in Radley's large hands.

"Hi," she croaked. She had to clear her throat and repeat the greeting.

"My mother had to go to work. She asked me to help you out while she's gone. I hope that's okay."

Olivia rose slowly, careful not to hurt her sore tummy, and stepped towards him. "Yes, of course. Thank you. I knew your mum was going out. I thought she'd call me inside before she went."

"Maybe she didn't bother because I'm here."

"I guess you're right."

Instinctively, Olivia reached to take her baby. She stepped up close to Radley and slid her fingers around George, but Radley didn't let go. There was an awkward moment when they both held him. The backs of Olivia's hands pressed against hard, masculine ribs. A little zing of awareness shot through her.

She hadn't noticed how tall Radley was when she first saw him, taller than Cameron by a couple of inches at least. His shoulders were broader and his muscles bigger. Everything about him was a bit more mature than Cameron. She looked up into his eyes, light brown tinged with green around the pupils. For a moment the world went away and there was only the three of them.

"Mum mentioned you shouldn't lift anything," Radley said softly.

"Oh, yes. I'd forgotten."

The spell broken, Olivia stepped back so fast she stumbled and had to grab the bench to catch her balance. Pain shot through her body and she winced.

"Careful, there." Radley was beside her in an instant.

He held George in one arm while his other came around her shoulders, steadying her. "Did you hurt yourself?"

"Not much. I'm fine. Sometimes I forget that I have to be careful."

As the ache faded, tears flooded Olivia's eyes. She blinked them away, but it was a losing battle. Drips fell over her lashes and ran down her cheeks. She'd tried to be strong, to cope alone, but it had been so tough sometimes. All she'd wanted was a little moral support from Cameron, just to know he was concerned about her welfare and would be there for George, so the little guy didn't grow up without a dad.

She'd pushed that worry down deep but the sight of George in Radley's arms and now his concern for her brought the longing back.

"Hey, no need for tears." Radley drew her closer and enfolded her against his chest. The stubble on his chin brushed her forehead. She laid her cheek on his firm, warm muscles and wiped her face on her sleeve. She had to stop crying. She was sobbing all over a man she barely knew, the brother of her baby's father. This was not the impression she wanted to give him. She should compose herself and pull away.

Instead she pressed closer, absorbing Radley's warmth and strength, safe for a few minutes in his embrace with her baby. She knew nothing about him except that he was an army doctor who'd just returned from Afghanistan, yet she sensed he was everything his mother had claimed, kind, gentle, and dependable. He was everything she'd hoped Cameron would be.

For a fleeting moment she wished Radley were George's father.

Olivia pulled away and Radley reluctantly released her. She had felt good in his arms. Too good. This woman had been his brother's girlfriend and had just given birth to a baby. She was about as off-limits as a woman could be.

Radley stepped back to increase the distance between them and tried to forget the feel of her womanly curves pressed against him. He cleared his throat and concentrated on changing his hold on George to give himself a few seconds.

The tiny boy chose that moment to wake up and let out a plaintive wail. It was good timing.

"Mum said you'd want to feed him now," Radley suggested.

"That's right. Can you bring him into the lounge for me? I find it most comfortable to feed him in the leather recliner by the French window."

"That's my father's chair." Radley smiled at the thought of a woman feeding a baby in the chair where his father liked to do the *Times* crossword.

"I know." Olivia kept pace with him as they wandered towards the house. "Your mum said Brigadier Knight wouldn't mind. I hope she's right. I met him when I was in the hospital before he went back to Afghanistan. I get the impression he doesn't stand for any nonsense."

Radley laughed. "That's why they want him over there to help supervise the closing down of some of the medical facilities before we withdraw. He gets people moving."

When they reached the back door, Radley stood aside and ushered Olivia through, then followed her along the hall to the sitting room. He hadn't noticed the state of the room when he'd first seen Olivia here. Now he saw how much baby paraphernalia lay around—a baby bed, blankets, toys, bags, tubes and pots of cream, and a plastic contraption that probably had something to do with feeding the child. The rather staid room with its velvet curtains and leather sofas even smelled of baby stuff.

George squirmed in Radley's arms and let out a high-pitched wail. "You've got a good set of lungs on you, young man." Radley glanced at Olivia as she gingerly sat down and made herself comfortable. "I think he's hungry."

"Yep. He's hungry most of the time. Your mum says he's trying to catch up because he was small at birth. I had to spend the last couple of months in the hospital. He wasn't growing fast enough."

"That can't have been much fun."

"No. I nearly went stir crazy." Olivia gathered her long dark hair and caught it back in a band from around her wrist. Then she placed a pillow on her lap and Radley laid George there.

"Do they know why he didn't put on weight?"

"I was really sick in the first few months. That meant I got so behind on my college work I had to study like mad to catch up as well as find time to earn money to pay the bills. Your mum thinks maybe a combination of me not keeping my food down and working too hard caused it."

And to think Radley had been concerned that Olivia was a lazy user like his ex-wife.

"Well, he might be a tad small, but he looks healthy." Radley picked up a huge tome from the floor beside her chair and checked the spine. It was a law text. "Yours?" he asked as he laid it on a table.

"Some of the work I still need to catch up on. I'm in the final year of my law degree, but I missed the exams. I'm taking them in November."

She had ambition. He approved of that.

Olivia untucked her top and turned those huge blue eyes on him. He didn't want to leave, but she was obviously waiting for him to go so she could start feeding.

"Anything you need?"

"A cup of coffee in about fifteen minutes would be

great."

Radley pulled the sitting room door closed behind him and caught a glimpse of her lifting her sweater. Something he shouldn't be feeling jolted through him. He turned away and pressed his lips together. Just treat her like a sister-in-law, he told himself. After all, if Cameron came back and married her, that's what she would be.

As he put on the coffee machine, he mulled over their conversation. He knew very little about her, but one thing was clear—she was nothing like his ex-wife. She appeared to be everything he wished his ex-wife *had* been, capable, hardworking, and ambitious. The sort of woman who would contribute to a marriage and not spend all her husband's money and run around behind his back getting pregnant by another man.

What puzzled him was why his brother had dumped her after he left college. Men in the military had long-distance relationships. It happened all the time. The stupid idiot obviously didn't have the experience to recognize a good thing when he had it.

It was time Radley set him straight and helped them get back together.

The sitting room was very quiet when Radley returned later with Olivia's cup of coffee. He pushed the door ajar and peered in. The recliner was tipped back, and it looked as though Olivia had fallen asleep holding George. Radley hurried in and set the cup down.

He need not have worried. George was snuggled safely in her arm on the pillow. He paused to take in the scene of mother and baby. There really was something magical about the sight. It was a shame Cameron was missing this, missing seeing his son so small. The child would grow quickly.

Careful not to disturb Olivia, he lifted the baby out of her arms, laid him in the bassinet at her side, and tucked him in. George's tiny fingers curled around Radley's thumb. He grinned for a moment before pulling his hand away. The kid already had a strong grip.

Fetching a fleecy blanket, he laid it over Olivia, then smoothed back some strands of hair that had come adrift from her ponytail. A healthy pink flush colored her skin and her thick eyelashes lay in dark crescents on her cheeks. Cameron really was an idiot to stay away. If this beautiful woman and her adorable baby boy belonged to Radley, nothing would keep him from them.

Olivia stirred and flickers of blue appeared between her lashes. "Is George all right?"

"He's fine. You sleep. I'll be around if you want me. Just call."

"Okay." Her eyelashes drifted closed again. He took another moment to watch her before turning away.

He ran upstairs to his room and fished his mobile phone out of his bag. It still had a little charge left—enough to make one call, anyway. He sat on the edge of his bed and scrolled through his contacts to his brother's number. Cameron was stationed in Germany, only one hour ahead of the UK.

As the phone rang, he stared out the window, down the garden to the pond where he'd found Olivia watching the ducks. He'd expected to get voice mail but his brother picked up.

"Hey, Rad, are you home?"

"I'm sitting on my bed, appreciating the silence."

"I suppose it's good to see the old place again. I should come home, but I can't wait to be stationed somewhere more exciting. It's all routine stuff in Germany."

Radley remembered thinking the same when he was first qualified and fresh out of the Royal Military Academy Sandhurst with his captain's pips. He had longed to be sent to a war zone where he could get more experience. He'd come down to earth with a bump when the first injured servicemen had arrived on his operating table. He'd always wanted to be a surgeon, but there was something soul-destroying about seeing men, day after day, who'd been harmed on purpose.

"Do you know where you're going?" he asked.

"No, only that I'll ship out after Christmas."

"You've got enough time to come home for a weekend then."

"Not really."

"I managed to get back here occasionally when I was stationed in Germany. You need to make the effort. Mum must have told you Olivia and her baby are staying here."

Silence greeted his comment.

"Come on, Cam. You must deal with this."

"I don't see how the baby's mine. We always used protection."

"News flash, mate, condoms aren't infallible."

Cameron's sigh hissed through the phone. "I'm still not convinced. You were the one who told me not to get suckered."

"That was before I met Olivia." Radley pinched the bridge of his nose. He'd known this would be a difficult conversation. "If she says George is yours, I believe her."

"She named the baby after Dad?"

"Yes."

More silence.

"Come home and see them. Olivia's had a tough time. It would do her good to know you care enough to visit your son. I guarantee that once you hold the little guy, you'll feel differently about this."

Cameron heaved another sigh. "You're sure he's mine?"

"He looks like you. Mum thinks so, and I suppose Dad does too or Olivia wouldn't be here."

Another frustrated sigh.

"So, you'll come?"

"I guess."

"Don't wait too long. George gets bigger every day."

"This stinks. I'm too young to have a kid. I've got plans."

"Olivia has plans as well. She's had to adapt. You can too."

Cameron grunted in response.

"Call Olivia and tell her when you're coming."

"Maybe. See you, man."

Radley flopped back on his bed and stared at the ceiling. Had he done the right thing? What would Olivia's reaction be if Cameron contacted her? A sense of regret washed through him, and he pushed it away. It was best for George to have his father in his life. It would also help Olivia to feel that she belonged in the family. Yet part of him wished he hadn't called his brother.

"We're going for a ride in my car. That'll be fun, won't it?" Radley jangled his keys over the baby in his arms to attract his gaze. George's arms and legs waved like crazy and he made the grunting sound that signaled he was excited.

If Radley had known beforehand that he would spend most of his time watching out for a mother and newborn when he arrived home on leave, he might have stayed away. But he enjoyed being with Olivia and George. He didn't even mind that his mother had a couple of weeks working full time to cover for a sick colleague, which meant that for the last week, Radley had been pretty much tied to the house all day.

At some point he needed to go house hunting for his own place, but that could wait. He had four weeks' leave after his tour of duty and eight weeks of regular leave that he hadn't taken, plenty of time to find somewhere.

A noise sounded on the stairs. He glanced up from his position by the front door to see Olivia descending. He snatched a breath and blew it out. His gaze trailed up long, slender legs. She always wore sweatpants in the house, but today she had on a blue dress that reached just above her knees. Man, did it suit her. "You look nice."

She stepped off the bottom step and approached, a tentative smile on her face. "It's the first time I've been out since your mum brought me and George home from the hospital. I know I'm only going back there for a checkup, but I thought I should make an effort."

Her long dark hair glided around her shoulders as she moved. Her eyes looked bigger than usual, outlined with makeup, while her glossy pink lips were far too tempting.

She must have noticed his appraisal. Her hand went to her mouth, and tiny lines appeared between her eyebrows. "I haven't overdone the makeup, have I? It's been such a long time since I wore any."

"No, you look great. I'm just not used to seeing it on you."

The tentative smile came back to her face. "That's okay, then." She turned her attention to her son. "Hi, sweetie. Are you being a good boy?"

In answer, the baby in Radley's arms farted loudly. Olivia burst out laughing and so did Radley. A moment later the baby noisily filled his diaper.

"That sounded like a seven or eight on the Richter scale," Radley said. "I reckon that was his loudest poo yet."

Olivia clutched her stomach. "Don't make me laugh. It hurts." When she had recovered, she wiped tears of laughter from her lashes. "Only a man would say something like that."

"I aim to please." Radley grinned, happy to have amused her. She was far too serious most of the time. If she wasn't looking after George, she had her head buried in a law book or her college notes. He admired her determination to pass her exams, but she needed to give herself a break sometime.

"Better out than in, I guess." Olivia turned back to the stairs. "If you carry him up, I'll change the dirty bottom."

Chapter Three

When Olivia finally stepped out the front door, after she'd changed George's diaper and most of his clothes, a practical family SUV stood on the gravel. "I expected you to own something sporty."

"I used to."

Olivia waited for more explanation, but that was all Radley said.

He opened the back door and settled George in the car seat, which was already fixed in place. He bent to fiddle with the straps. "How the heck does this thing fasten?"

Olivia bit back her laugh. She didn't mention that it had taken her and Radley's mother a good ten minutes to figure out the fastenings when they first put George in the seat.

She squeezed into the doorway beside Radley. He angled his body to give her room and she ended up with her shoulder against his chest. She blinked slowly, a little dazed by his spicy masculine fragrance. She loved being close to him. There was something about him that drew her like the proverbial moth to a flame. She enjoyed his touch when he took George from her arms and the times he'd put his arm around her waist or shoulders.

"Are you going to strap him in, or do you plan to just

stand here all day. Not that I'm complaining."

"Sorry, I was thinking." Olivia's face heated. She bent her head over her son and snapped the plastic clips together.

"Ah, I see. Easy when you know how."

She stepped aside. Radley's hand rested warm and firm on her back while he opened the front passenger door for her.

George went to sleep once the car moved off, and they drove in silence for a few minutes. Olivia glanced at Radley's tight expression. She'd spent a lot of time with him this past week. He was generally chatty and friendly, very easy to get along with. This was the first occasion she'd seen him like this. She hoped he wasn't getting tired of having to help her. The poor man had hardly had a moment to himself since he arrived home.

"Is something the matter?"

He glanced at her as if he'd forgotten she was there. "Just lost in the past."

"Not a happy past by the look of it."

"No."

She waited, hoping for more.

After a few moments he laughed wearily. "I was married. Did you know that?"

"Your mum mentioned you were divorced."

"My wife was pregnant."

Trepidation shot through Olivia. If something bad had happened to Radley's child, then expecting him to help her with George was unfair. It must bring back sad memories. "I didn't know. What happened?"

"Turns out the baby wasn't mine."

"Oh, Radley. I'm sorry." Olivia laid a hand on his arm. The pain in his eyes pinched her heart. The woman must have been a fool to cheat on a good man like Radley. She'd give a lot to find a husband as considerate as him.

"This car always reminds me. I bought it to bring my

baby home from the hospital." He glanced over his shoulder at George. "At least it's finally proving useful."

"I'm sorry we've brought back such painful memories. If you'd rather not help me with George anymore, I'll understand. I'm sure I can manage."

"Don't be daft. You've still got weeks until you can drive or lift anything." Radley rubbed a hand over his face. "Anyway, I like helping you."

"Okay, if you're sure."

He nodded.

They drove the rest of the way in awkward silence.

Radley wove the car through the traffic, turned into the hospital gate, and found a parking space. He cut the engine and flipped the keys over in his hand. "Look, forget I mentioned my wife. I'm not sure why I did. I don't normally talk about her."

Before Olivia could answer he stepped out of the car and moved to the trunk to retrieve George's stroller. She supervised while he lifted her baby from the car and loaded the stroller with the baby essentials.

After a short walk and elevator ride, they reached the clinic. She checked in and they found seats in the waiting area. A few minutes later, the doctor who had delivered George stepped out of a consulting room and called her name. The pretty blonde doctor came towards them and held out her hand. "My goodness, Radley, how are you?"

"Tina. I didn't know you were working here." They shook hands.

Olivia's doctor nodded towards George. "Is he your son?"

"No, my brother's."

Tina smiled with what looked like relief. "We should meet for a drink and catch up. I'd love to hear about your experiences as an army doctor. I might consider joining up myself."

"Okay, sounds like a good idea. Give me your

number. I'll call you."

Olivia folded her arms as the blonde doctor reeled off a number while Radley tapped it into his phone.

"I'd better get on or I'll be behind. See you soon," the woman said to Radley. Then she beckoned Olivia inside.

"I'll keep an eye on George," Radley said with a smile.

Olivia followed the tall blonde into the consulting room. In the past, she hadn't paid much attention to what the doctor looked like, but the woman was quite pretty, and blonde, of course. Men liked blondes. She slumped down in the chair.

The doctor examined her tummy and pronounced that she was healing well. The bruising was still evident but starting to fade, and it was less sore.

"Another four weeks and you should be back to normal. Is the father around to help you?"

"No, Cameron's in Germany." Olivia didn't tell her that they hadn't spoken for months.

"I feel comfortable handing your care over to your general practitioner now. I'll write to Dr. Knight and let her know. Are you still staying with her?"

"The plan is for me to stay with the Knights until the New Year. By then I will be back on my feet and ready to cope alone."

"Good. And you've got Radley to help. He's a great guy. Do you know if he's seeing anyone right now?"

Olivia was tempted to lie, but she couldn't bring herself to do it. Tina had always been nice to her and was a good doctor. She might be just what Radley needed to move forward and put the past behind him. "I don't think so."

"Great. I've had a thing for him since college." She laughed and laid a hand on Olivia's arm. "Don't tell him that."

Olivia mimed zipping her lips.

"Thanks."

They both stood, and Tina saw her to the door. "Take it easy and enjoy your baby for a few more weeks before you do anything too demanding."

Olivia smiled and nodded.

Back outside, Radley rose to his feet as she approached. "All okay?"

"I think so. She doesn't want to see me again."

"That's good. Let's get you two home. George is gnawing his fist."

"Uh-oh. We only have a few minutes before he starts crying for his food."

As they traveled down in the elevator, Olivia couldn't stop herself questioning Radley about Tina. "Are you going to take Tina up on her invitation?"

"I might. We were at college together. I didn't know her well, but she's an okay sort. If she's thinking of joining the army, I should make the effort to give her some time."

Mentioning the army was just a line to get him interested, Olivia longed to say. Could he not see that? She drew in a breath and let it go. She mustn't interfere in Radley's private life. What he did in the evening was none of her business.

"Have some more bacon. You need to eat plenty while you're breast-feeding." Sandra leaned over Olivia with strips of bacon balanced on a spatula, ready to put them on her plate.

"Gosh, no thank you. I'm full, honestly." The kitchen table was laden with toast, butter, jam, fruit juices, yogurt, and breakfast cereals—a normal thing in the Knight household. Radley seemed to eat like a horse, although where he put it she didn't know. There wasn't an ounce of fat on the man, probably because he was up early every day running.

Sandra turned to Radley and dumped the rest of the

bacon on his plate. He didn't seem to notice, his attention was fixed on the real estate listing of houses for sale. Every morning details arrived in the mail from real estate agents and every morning he leafed through them and tossed them in the trash.

After a few moments he sat back with a sigh. "I've changed my mind. I don't want an apartment. They all look like prison cells. I'm going to try and find a place around here."

"If you end up working at the local military hospital, it'll take around forty minutes to get in during rush hour. You know that, don't you?" Sandra said.

"I don't care about the commute. I want a decent house with a garden and at least three bedrooms."

His mother frowned as she took her seat and buttered some toast. "Do you have a family tucked away somewhere I don't know about?"

"I will someday. If I'm going to buy a place, I want it to be future proof."

"Makes sense, I guess," Olivia said, although she didn't like the thought of Radley with a wife and children. But it would happen one day so she'd have to get used to the idea.

He tore open the last envelope and pulled out another property detail sheet. "This is more like it." He perused the paper then gave it to his mother, who nodded as she chewed.

"Can you afford this much?"

"Yes."

He retrieved the paper and laid it beside Olivia's plate. "What do you think?"

The place was a pretty cottage with a fountain in the front garden and a long backyard that appeared to have a field on one side and woodland on the other. It was her dream home. If only she could afford somewhere like this, somewhere George would grow up with plenty of room to play, where he wouldn't be breathing in horrid city fumes that might give him asthma.

The thought reinforced her determination to pass her exams and secure an internship at a good law practice. As a successful lawyer, in a few years she would be able to buy a home like this for her son.

"It's lovely. I think you should check it out."

"Want to come with me?" Radley tossed his napkin on the table and stood. "I'm going to head on over there today and look at the outside."

Olivia's heart jumped, then fell. "I can't. I've only got a few weeks left before my exams. I need to work."

"Ease up on yourself," Sandra said. "It's Saturday and a lovely day for this time of year. Take a break."

Olivia was tempted, really tempted. She wanted to see the cottage so she could visualize it and imagine the place was hers. That would give her even more incentive to work hard and make the dream a reality. She also wanted to spend time with Radley.

"Come on, Livi." Radley smiled down at her. "You know you want to."

"Oh, all right."

"Great. You prep George. I'll bring the car around."

An hour later, after George had been changed, fed, and changed again, she finally had him ready. Radley carried him out and secured him in the baby seat. Then they set off for the village of Fordbridge.

They drove along pretty country lanes bordered by hedges. Some hardy wildflowers still dotted the hedgerows with color, even though the weather had turned cold and they'd woken to a crisp frost that morning.

"Fordbridge is on the canal." Radley pointed as they rounded a bend and the waterway came into view. Long colorful barges of blue, green, and red lined the bank. "When we were kids, Cam and I used to cycle out here to fish. We would sneak onto the vacant barges sometimes as well. They're rented by vacationers in the summer, but most of them are moored up and left empty in the cold weather."

Olivia tried to imagine Cameron and Radley as boys, cycling along the canal towpath, and fishing together. She found she could quite easily. Cameron had behaved like a big kid in college so she didn't need to stretch her imagination far.

"Here's the village." Radley glanced around as the country lane wound between some picturesque stone cottages. "It's so long since I was here I'd forgotten what the place is like. Check the directions on the realtor's details."

Olivia dug in the bag at her feet and pulled out the sheet of paper. "Take a right after the Hunter's Moon Pub. Then we should see the property on the right. It sounds as though it's on the edge of the village."

The pub was an ancient beamed building that had probably stood at the center of the village since Elizabethan times. "I like the look of that," Radley said as he slowed to take the turn. "Hope it's walking distance from the house."

A couple of minutes later he eased up on the gas and stopped. The cottage was as pretty as the picture, with roses over the door and a tiny stone fountain on the patch of lawn. A sign on the gate read BROOK VIEW COTTAGE.

When the car stopped, George woke and made his excited grunting sound. "There, see, the little guy likes it already."

Olivia gave Radley an eye roll, but she smiled as well. "It is a cute place."

"Don't call it cute, please," Radley said. "Guys don't buy cute places."

"Okay, quaint."

"Better. I can do quaint. That has an old-fashioned ring to it."

Radley came around her side of the car and lifted

George out of his car seat. The tiny boy curled his fists in Radley's sweater and pumped his legs. "You are such a funny little guy." Radley kissed the top of George's head. Olivia's stomach did its usual flip when she saw the two of them together.

They went through the front gate, and Radley knocked on the door.

"Shouldn't you call the agent?"

"Probably."

Nobody answered the door so Radley wandered to a window and peered inside. "The place looks empty."

Olivia joined him and cupped her hands around her face so she could see through the glass. "There's no furniture. Maybe it's a bank repossession. If it is, you might get a good deal."

"I'd like to see inside before I get carried away." Radley shifted George into one arm and dug his mobile phone out of his pocket. He dialed the number on the realtor's sign outside the property. A few minutes later, he'd arranged for an agent to show them the house in two hours' time.

"How about lunch at the Hunter's Moon? Let's check it out. It might be my local soon."

"Sure. The place looked nice from the outside." Olivia rested a hand on Radley's shoulder and leaned closer to nuzzle her son's cheek. She loved kissing her baby boy, and it was a good excuse to get close to Radley as well. "As soon as we've eaten I need to feed Georgie Porgie again."

"Let's hope he makes it through our lunch without crying. Perhaps we'd better hurry up."

Radley strapped George back in his seat, and they drove the two minutes to the pub. The car park was packed but he managed to slide his car in a space at the end of a row.

The hum of cheerful voices greeted them as they entered the side door. "Do you think it's all right to

31

bring a baby in?" Olivia said, scanning the old wooden bar with its low-beamed ceiling. Cozy chairs flanked a roaring log fire. Although the place was busy, she couldn't see any other children.

"Should be fine as long as we don't let him drink."

Olivia playfully punched Radley's arm, and he burst out laughing.

They ordered drinks at the bar. The barman directed them through to a restaurant area at the back. It turned out to be a light, airy extension with big windows overlooking the canal.

"Wow, I've never seen so many barges in one place." Olivia halted by a window and stared out at a channel divided off from the main canal. It was packed solid with watercraft.

"I hadn't realized the pub looked out over here." Radley pointed to a group of stone buildings on the edge of the water. "That's the head office of the barge rental business."

They took a window table. Radley had carried George in his car seat and he set it on the floor beside Olivia's chair. "Hey, sweetie, are you going to be a good boy and let Mummy have her lunch?" She ran her fingers over George's soft, dark hair. He kicked his feet and grunted.

She'd attached a yellow flashing star-shaped baby toy to the carry handle of the seat. George fixed his blue eyes on it and stretched out a hand.

"Look at that. It's the first time I've seen him reach for something." Radley left his seat and crouched beside George. "Clever boy, Georgie." Radley tapped the star to make its light flash again.

A murmur of yearning escaped Olivia's lips. She felt an almost unbearable longing to wrap her arms around Radley and hold on so tight he could never get away. In the last four weeks she'd spent a lot of time with him and often needed his help. He had never let her down or complained, even when George's cries woke him in the middle of the night.

Radley was kind, gentle, and patient. Her initial attraction to him had grown into something far more. The thought of being parted from him sent a pulse of pain through her. She was falling in love with him, and she had no idea how to handle it. If he were anyone else it might work, but he was Cameron's brother.

The waitress approached. Radley reclaimed his seat and ordered a steak. Olivia ordered pasta. While they ate, they chatted about what Radley was looking for in a home.

"You all right?" he asked after a while. "You seem distracted."

Olivia shrugged. The internal conflict between her attraction to Radley and her self-reproach had grown steadily from the first day she met him.

She longed to tell him her feelings, but how could she when she'd just given birth to his brother's child? He'd probably be disgusted with her. And if he wasn't, his mother and father surely would be. She respected his parents and valued their good opinion. They were too important a part of George's life for her to fall out with them.

Olivia drew in a breath and released it slowly. She had to stop longing for Radley and get over it. He would always be in her life, but as George's uncle.

As if he sensed her disquiet, George let out a wail. Olivia had nearly finished her meal and appreciated the excuse to take a break from Radley to compose herself.

"Lunchtime for you now, sweetie." She reached down and stroked George's cheek. How she longed to be able to pick her baby up instead of depending on others.

Radley immediately got up and lifted the baby seat. "Come on, munchkin." He turned a smile on Olivia. "I'll take him to the car, then come back and pay."

When George was fed and changed, they returned to Brook View Cottage to meet the real estate agent. Radley had bought a baby carrier so he could hold George on his chest and have his hands free. He sat in the back of the car, Olivia beside him. Together they managed to get George into the carrier while it was on Radley's lap.

"Now comes the tricky part." Radley held the baby in place while Olivia moved to adjust the clips at his neck and waist, altering the length of the straps and securing the carrier. She closed the one at his waist and wedged a knee underneath herself to get a better angle to reach the higher one.

Her hand brushed the smooth skin of Radley's neck above his sweater and she trailed the tips of her fingers across his hair. She longed to lean forward and press her lips against his skin, to wrap her arms around this wonderful man and her little boy.

So she did. Not kiss him—that would have been too daring. But when the carrier was secure, she folded her arms around Radley, rested her chin on his shoulder, and leaned forward to see George's little pink face, almost lost in the hood of his padded romper suit and Radley's sweater.

She breathed in Radley's clean fragrance and stroked her little boy's back. A strong masculine hand rose and cupped her cheek. For long moments they both remained still and silent. Olivia hardly dared breathe for fear she'd break the spell.

"Livi," he said softly. "I've grown very fond of you."

He turned his head and his warm breath touched her face. She snuggled closer to him and her eyelids fell. "Me too," she whispered. It was on the tip of her tongue to say more, to give away how deeply she really felt for him, when George gave a familiar burp and the smell of partly digested milk filled the car.

"Oh, no, you didn't, Georgie." Olivia could hardly

bear to look.

"Oops." Radley scrunched up his nose at the sight of milky vomit on the front of his sweater. "Way to ruin the mood, pal."

"Yikes, sorry." Olivia scrambled for the baby bag, dug out the wet wipes, and mopped up the worst of the mess. Her darling little boy was certainly no matchmaker. But perhaps the interruption had been for the best. She'd been about to say something she might regret.

As they finished cleaning up, a small red car pulled in behind them. A woman in a navy suit climbed out. They both scrambled from the vehicle, Radley with a protective arm around George in his baby carrier.

"Mr. and Mrs. Knight." The realtor strode forward, hand out. "I'm Lindsey Phelps."

"We're not married," Olivia said, hastening to put her right. "I'm just along for the ride today."

"Oh, I see." The pretty young woman's smile grew wider as her gaze swept over Radley. "Love the accessory. All good-looking men should wear a baby. Makes you look doubly cute."

Radley opened his mouth then closed it again, obviously taken aback by the woman's comment. "Shall we go in?" he said. "I'm eager to look around."

"Of course."

Lindsey unlocked the door, then stood aside to let them pass. They wandered through the empty house, opening cupboards and looking out of windows. The place had a slight musty smell from being unoccupied, but it had huge potential. With a makeover it would be an adorable family home.

After they had been upstairs to check out the bedrooms and bathroom, the realtor unlocked the back door and they explored the long backyard. At the bottom was a strong wooden fence that bordered the canal towpath.

"Wow, this is a fantastic location," Olivia said. The views from the upstairs windows all looked out over lovely countryside, and it was within walking distance of the village shop as well as the pub.

"It's a pretty cottage in a wonderful position." Lindsey handed Radley a brochure with more photos and details inside. "We do have other people interested, so don't wait too long if you want to make an offer."

"Great, thank you. I'll think about it and may be in touch."

Radley didn't say any more until they were back in the car, George settled in his car seat. He waited for Lindsey to lock up and drive away, then turned in his seat to face Olivia. "What do you think?"

"Great potential." As she said the words, images scrolled through her mind of the various rooms redecorated and furnished as she would do them if the place were hers. "I like it."

Radley nodded slowly and bit his lip. "I agree. I'm going to make an offer." He flipped over the brochure and checked the price. It had already been marked down by quite a few thousand. "I don't want to appear too eager. I'll wait until Monday, then offer twenty thousand less than they're asking."

"Good plan." Olivia stretched her lips into a smile but she couldn't stop the wave of sadness inside. One day Radley would live here with another woman and have a family. She and George would visit, and he'd probably joke about the day they came here together to view the place.

The thought brought tears to her eyes.

Chapter Four

Radley jolted awake and glanced at the bedside clock. He was used to being woken in the early hours of the morning by George, but the baby was silent. It must be his dreams that had pulled him from his sleep.

The owners of Brook View Cottage had accepted his offer to purchase a few days ago. With luck the place would be his by Christmas, but ever since he'd seen the cottage he'd been plagued by a recurring dream.

He threw an arm over his eyes and tried to drift back to sleep, but memories of what was really a nightmare kept repeating in his head.

He was in the hospital with his wife, holding his unnamed baby boy in his arms while his wife looked on adoringly. Then a man came into the room and took the baby from him. His wife cast him a derisive look and fell into the man's arms. Then they walked out, leaving Radley alone in the white room.

Next the scenario altered. Radley was in his new house with Olivia and George. Cameron came through the front door, and Olivia ran into his arms. He picked up George and they all left, leaving Radley alone again.

It was crazy. The situations weren't the same at all, but deep down the same fear assailed him. He would lose the woman and baby he now thought of as his own.

A snuffling cry sounded from Olivia's room, the

noise George made when he had been sucking his fist for a while and was getting really hungry. In a few moments he would be screaming.

Radley welcomed the distraction. He tossed aside his covers, pulled on a robe, then padded barefoot along the corridor to the next bedroom. The door stood ajar so he pushed it and peered in.

Olivia still lay in bed, her dark hair spread across the pillow. She turned her head and smiled sleepily his way. Radley slipped inside, closing the door behind him so his mother wasn't disturbed by the noise, and moved to stand over George's bassinet. "Hey, hungry boy. Shall we pass you over to Mummy?"

He lifted George and cuddled him. "You ready, Liv?"

"Give me a moment." Olivia climbed out of bed, wrapped a fleecy pink robe around herself, and headed for the bathroom.

"Time for us to change your bum, young man." Radley laid George on the changing unit, removed the wet diaper, and, with the ease of much practice, wiped George's bottom clean and wrapped on a new one. While he waited for Olivia to return, he massaged George's feet. The little boy fell silent and stared up at Radley, his eyes glazed.

Olivia returned, heaped her pillows behind her and settled, ready to take her son. Radley normally left her to breast-feed alone, but this time he passed George across and sat on the end of the bed. He wanted to share this moment.

"All right if I stay?"

She hesitated for a second before nodding.

Radley averted his gaze while Olivia pulled down the front of her nightie and latched George on her breast. When she settled, he glanced at her again. The little boy was sucking away, his tiny hands flattened against her skin.

"George loves having his feet rubbed," he said.

"Who doesn't?" she said with a laugh.

Her response gave him an idea. He folded aside the covers and found one of her slender, pale feet. He cradled the heel in his palm, and worked his thumbs over her sole.

"Ah, that's heaven." Olivia dropped her head back on the pillows and her eyelids fell.

Radley admired her while she wasn't looking but returned his gaze to her foot as soon as she opened her eyes. He continued to work on her toes as George fed. When Olivia switched her baby to the other breast, Radley moved over to massage her other foot.

Little moans of pleasure whispered between her lips, moans that fired his nerves and set his blood pumping. He wanted to be with this woman, and he wanted to be there for George. But what about Cameron? His frustrated emotions welled up. Cameron didn't deserve her after the way he'd behaved. His irresponsible brother still hadn't bothered to contact Olivia. She deserved so much better; she deserved to be loved and cherished. Radley lifted Olivia's foot and pressed his lips against her instep.

The sounds of pleasure stopped abruptly. Silence filled the room. Radley raised his gaze to find her eyes wide. He'd gone too far, offended her. Until now their contact had been affectionate, like siblings. Kissing her had changed things.

"I'm sorry." Radley climbed off the bed and pulled the covers back over her feet. "I should go."

"No." She extended a hand. He took it and sat beside her. She'd finished feeding George, and had the child resting on her shoulder while she patted his back. Radley gathered the sleepy boy in his arms and deposited him in his bassinet.

Instead of leaving he returned to Olivia and took her hand again. "I want to sleep with you."

Her breath rushed in on a soft hiss of surprise. "I'm

not ready for anything like that, Radley."

"No..." Radley winced and shook his head. He needed to choose his words more carefully. "I mean literally, not euphemistically. I just want to hold you in my arms." That was actually a lie. He wanted a lot more eventually, but one step at a time.

She appeared to think for a moment, then slid over and turned back the covers. Radley's heart pounded as he climbed into bed beside her and snuggled down, drawing her warm, slender form into his arms. She wriggled closer, her hands on his chest, and gave a contented little whimper.

Every cell in Radley's body fired to life. He wasn't sure he'd get a wink of sleep, but it would be worth lying awake for the rest of the night to be with Olivia.

This was a difficult situation yet he'd make it work out. He'd wait for the right moment to tell his mother how he felt about Olivia, then he'd call Cameron and explain. If his brother had been interested in Olivia, it would be different. But he hadn't bothered to contact her, even though Radley had encouraged him. After all this time, it was safe to assume his brother wasn't coming back to claim her or his son.

Olivia woke to the flicker of sunlight across her face, immediately aware of a solid, warm body spooning her from behind.

Radley. What had happened in the early hours of the morning rushed back on a wave of excitement—the foot rubbing, the way he'd watched her while she fed George, the way he'd asked permission to stay the rest of the night in bed with her, to hold her.

And he was holding her still, his arm curled over her ribs, his large, strong hand covering hers.

She had hoped he returned her feelings but not dared to believe it until now.

She flexed her hand beneath his, just to feel the slide

of his palm across her skin. His fingers tightened around hers, and her breath caught. His shallow, even breathing had made her think he was still asleep.

"Good morning," he whispered.

She felt him shift and looked over her shoulder. He'd boosted himself up on his elbow to smile down at her. "Turn around, Livi. We need to talk before George wakes up."

They did need to talk, but she didn't want to have this conversation now, the one where they discussed all the reasons why they shouldn't be together. She just wanted to enjoy the sensation of his closeness and dream for a little longer. Despite her reluctance she rolled over to face him.

They lay for a few moments, heads on the pillows, faces barely twelve inches apart. Then Radley shifted forward and pressed his lips to hers. The kiss took her by surprise but her eyelids fell and she kissed him back, putting all her pent-up feelings into those few seconds before he withdrew.

"I shouldn't have done that." Radley's breath trailed out on a gentle sigh. "I shouldn't have slept with you, not until we'd handled the obstacles between us. I've put the cart in front of the horse, or something like that." He winced. "I don't think I've ever said that in my life before. It's one of those strange things Mum says. I'm really making a mess of this, aren't I?"

This strong, capable man was nervous. It sent a burst of warmth through her, warmth and love. She pulled her hand out from beneath the covers and placed her palm on his cheek, caressing his stubbly skin. "I love you."

There, she'd said the words that had been riding the back of her tongue for the last couple of weeks. Words that wanted to spill out every time Radley gently picked up George as though he were the most precious thing in the world, and kissed him with a complete lack of self-consciousness. He was a man comfortable in his own skin with nothing to prove, a man who seemed to find pleasure in helping those in need.

It was amazing he was Cameron's brother because they couldn't be more different. Cameron was focused on himself. She had trouble imagining how he'd empathize with his patients. Maybe the army would make him grow up and change.

Radley's fingers stroked her jaw, her cheek, her lips, his gaze following their course with an almost reverential look. "I think I fell in love with you the first time I set eyes on you. You were sitting in my father's chair with George at your breast. Seeing you there was almost a spiritual experience."

Olivia laughed, slightly embarrassed. "I suspect you're remembering it through rose-colored glasses."

Radley simply smiled and stroked strands of hair off her forehead.

"We need to tell your mum." This was what Olivia dreaded. She had such a good relationship with Sandra. She didn't want to spoil it.

"Let me break the news. I'll choose the right moment. Mum's down-to-earth and reasonable. She knows things don't always turn out as planned. And she can hardly be surprised when we've spent so much time together while Cameron hasn't even bothered to contact you."

Radley rolled on his back to stare at the ceiling. "There's something I need to tell you."

The change in his tone and expression sent a frisson of warning skating through Olivia. "It's nothing bad, is it?"

"You'll have to be the judge of that." Radley ran a hand over his face, and the moment stretched, pulling Olivia's nerves tight.

"In the interest of full disclosure, I have to admit that it's partly my fault Cameron didn't contact you when you told him you were pregnant."

"What?" How could that be? She hadn't even known Radley back then.

Radley turned to face her again. "Cam called me as soon as you contacted him about it. He was certain he couldn't have gotten you pregnant. I suggested that if he was really sure, he forget it and get on with his life."

Pain and disappointment spiked through Olivia. A sudden need for space made her roll away. She turned her back on him and chewed the side of her finger, trying to think.

"If I'd thought there was a chance he really was your baby's father, I'd have advised him to do the right thing. But he was so certain, Olivia."

Her initial shocked reaction faded and her rational mind caught hold again. Radley hadn't forced Cameron to ignore her. Cameron hadn't told Radley the truth, and it was Cameron's responsibility to make his own decisions. Cameron's behavior wasn't Radley's fault. To be honest, she was now relieved things had worked out this way or she would never have come to know Radley this well.

"In my defense, I did call him as soon as I came home and met you. I encouraged him to come and visit to see you and George."

Olivia pressed her fingers against her lips. Was it terrible to hope that Cameron ignored Radley's call? If he came back now intending to be a father to George, it might spoil any chance of her and Radley making a future together. That was what she wanted, even though she had only been with him for four weeks. Already she felt she knew him better than she'd ever known his brother.

Olivia rolled over and wrapped her arm around Radley, snuggling close. His breath whooshed out in relief, and he hugged her tightly against him.

"Are we good?" he said.

"We're good."

He kissed her again. "Now I just have to tell Mum."

"Speak to your mother before she goes out," Olivia said to Radley as they descended the stairs for breakfast. It had been four days since Radley first slept with Olivia. He'd stayed in her room every night since, simply holding her in his arms.

Of course, Sandra knew Radley visited Olivia's room at night to help with George, but she didn't know he slept there as well. Olivia hated being less than honest with her.

"Give me a few minutes alone with her. It's been impossible to pin her down this week while she's working."

Olivia wondered if she should have broached the subject with Sandra. She'd had more chances than Radley. She often studied at the kitchen table while Sandra prepared dinner. At this time Radley was usually occupied changing or bathing George. This final week before her exams, Olivia had hardly taken her head out of her notes. Radley had done everything for George except feed him.

As far as Olivia was concerned, the wretched exams couldn't be over soon enough. She wanted to claim her life back and spend time with her son. Whenever she heard Radley and George together, she longed to be with them rather than in the company of law books.

She had to keep reminding herself that these few weeks of study could set the course for her whole future. A good grade meant a training contract with a prestigious law firm; a low grade meant a less desirable firm or maybe even no training contract at all.

After the work she'd put in to reach this stage, she couldn't drop the ball now. Her future career was far too important for both her and George.

"I'm off to my Pilates class in fifteen minutes,"

Sandra shouted from the kitchen as Radley and Olivia reached the hall. "Breakfast is on the table for you two."

"Hang on, Mum. I need to have a word." Radley shot Olivia a glance, then strode along the hall, George still clutched in his arms.

Olivia paced back and forth, then turned and headed into the lounge. She busied herself tidying the space around the chair where she breast-fed. Surely Radley's mother wouldn't be surprised by the fact he and Olivia had fallen in love. She'd seen them together numerous times. Their growing affection must be apparent. To be honest, she had thrown them together in fairly intimate circumstances. It was partly Sandra's fault.

The house phone chimed and Olivia's heart jumped. "Blast." Bad timing. Radley only had a few minutes to talk to his mother. If she broke off to answer the phone, he'd have even less time.

The phone kept ringing and Olivia wandered into the hall to see what was happening. Sandra dashed out of the kitchen and snatched up the hall handset. "Hello." She swiped back her hair, looking flustered. "Cameron, darling, how wonderful to hear from you."

Olivia's gaze jumped to Radley, who had followed his mother. "Did you tell her?" Olivia mouthed silently.

Radley shook his head.

Olivia wrung her hands together. Why hadn't they found time to tell Sandra before Cameron called? This was bound to make it harder.

Meanwhile, Sandra was chatting away with Cameron. "Sorry if I sound a little out of breath. I couldn't find the handset in the kitchen so I had to dash out to the hall. Anyway, you don't want to know all that, do you. How are you, darling? Are you coming home?"

A tense silence filled the room as Olivia waited for the response.

"You are. Wonderful. I can't wait to hear how you're

getting along, and there's a tiny person here who's just dying to meet you... Yes, he's definitely your son."

Olivia's heart fell. Radley turned away and headed back to the kitchen.

"Olivia's standing right here. Have a word with her. I've got to rush off or I'll be late. See you next weekend."

Next weekend! Olivia squeezed her eyes closed for a long second, then forced a smile as Sandra offered her the phone. She took it reluctantly and placed it to her ear.

"Cameron."

"Hey, Livi, how are you?" He sounded cheerful and carefree. She'd gone through so much worry and pain to bring his son into the world while Cameron had been oblivious. Resentment flashed inside her, and she bit back a less-than-friendly retort.

"Very tired. I'm still healing from the emergency C-section, I have a newborn baby to care for, and I'm studying like mad because my exams begin the day after tomorrow."

"Yes. I'm sorry I didn't get back to you sooner. I've been busy."

"In all these months you haven't had one moment to contact me?"

Cameron cleared his throat. "I did post on your Facebook wall a few days ago to say I hoped things were going well, and that I'd call."

Olivia dropped down on the chair beside the telephone table and rested her head in her hand. "Checking social media is the last thing on my mind right now." Cameron really had no idea what looking after a baby was like. "You're coming for a visit?"

"I'll be back late on Friday. So that's good timing, you'll have just finished your finals, won't you? On Saturday night we can go out on the town to celebrate."

"What about George?"

"Oh, you mean the baby. Why did you have to give him Dad's name? That's really confusing."

"Nobody else seems to think so. Your dad was flattered."

"Yeah, I suppose he would be."

"You haven't answered the question, Cam. We can't just go out and abandon George. Anyway, I thought you'd want to spend time with your son."

"There'll be plenty of time for me to see him. I don't have to leave until Sunday afternoon. Mum can babysit on Saturday, can't she?"

"Your mum's been doing a lot of babysitting. So's Radley."

Cameron laughed. "Rad with a baby? I'd love to see that."

"I expect you will." Olivia didn't join in his laughter. She couldn't be less amused if she tried.

"Okay, see you Friday. Good luck with the exams."

"Thanks, Cam. Safe journey."

Olivia sat staring at the phone for a long time after the call ended. After months of praying Cameron would contact her and come to visit, this was now the last thing she wanted.

She glanced up, wondering where Radley had disappeared to. Sandra had left and the house seemed very quiet. She headed to the kitchen to find it empty and went to the window. Radley was out in the garden, George in his arms, standing looking out over the pond. He was so still that it set her nerves jangling. The situation with Cameron must be as difficult for him as it was for her. How would he handle it?

Chapter Five

This was Radley's nightmare come true. Yet he shouldn't be surprised. It had always been possible that Cameron would grow a conscience and shoulder his responsibilities. Only a month ago, Radley himself had encouraged Cameron to return to see Olivia and meet his son. How things had changed since then.

Radley smoothed his hand up and down the back of the precious little boy in his arms, the little boy he now thought of as his own. But George had never been Radley's. He was Cameron's son, and Olivia had been Cameron's girlfriend.

Radley was the interloper here, not Cameron.

"Rad, you okay?"

He turned at the sound of Olivia's voice and dragged his fingers through his hair. No, he wanted to say. I'm not okay. But this was tough for her. He wouldn't make the situation more difficult. "I'm fine. I've handled worse. When's Cam coming?"

"Next weekend."

"At least you'll have finished your exams."

"I guess. But the thought of his visit will occupy my mind."

"Yeah. Mine too."

She stopped beside him. They both stared at the ducks for a while. The chilly November wind cut through Radley's sweater. He'd wrapped a blanket around George, but he cuddled the little boy closer and put his other arm over Olivia's shoulders to keep her warm. "We should go in. You and George will get cold."

He took her hand, and they wandered back along the gravel path between flower borders, now bare after the summer flowers had been pulled up.

"Look, I've been thinking," Radley started. "Perhaps it's best if I go away for a couple of days while Cam's here. Give the two of you some space."

Olivia's startled gaze jumped to his face. She halted. "You're going to run out at the first obstacle."

"No." Was that what he was doing? "No," he said with more certainty. He didn't want to be here to see her with Cameron, but it was more than that. "It's only fair I give you two some time alone. If I'm here, it'll muddy the waters."

"Fair for who?"

Mainly Cameron, he realized. His little brother. Radley had hijacked his brother's girlfriend and baby. That had not been an issue all the while Cameron stayed away, but if he wanted to be a father to George and maybe even rekindle his relationship with Olivia, Radley must step back and give him a chance. He wouldn't do to Cameron what had been done to him.

"All of you," he said. "What if when Cam comes back you realize you still love him? You must have had strong feelings for him once."

"I never loved him like I love you."

A flash of relief mingled with guilt had Radley pulling Olivia into his arms. "I love you, sweetheart, I love you so much. I want to be with you and George more than anything else in the world."

And if he were really honest with himself, that was the main reason he had to go away this weekend. He couldn't bear to be here if Olivia did decide she still had feelings for Cameron.

***

"Please don't go." Olivia watched Radley folding ropes and checking clips and other bits and pieces of his climbing gear.

"I'll only be gone for a couple of days. I'll be home on Monday. Then we can discuss how you feel after Cam's visit."

"I know how I feel. I've told you. I love you. Cameron coming back is not going to change that."

Radley stuffed his climbing equipment in a sports bag and carried it out the front door. Olivia followed him. "I need you here, Radley." She knew he thought he was doing the right thing by giving her and Cameron space, but she couldn't help feeling he was deserting her just when she needed him most.

Since Cameron's phone call, Radley had pulled back from her. He hadn't spent the night with her this week, claiming she needed to sleep well because of her exams. She didn't buy that excuse.

"You don't need me to lift George anymore," Radley said as if purposely misunderstanding her.

He went to the massive black motorcycle parked on the gravel drive. She didn't know he owned a motorcycle until he brought the thing around to the front door fifteen minutes ago. She'd spent so much time with him over the last six weeks that she felt like she knew him inside out, but she obviously didn't. The realization unnerved her. Was he not the man she'd thought him to be?

He'd been on leave staying in his parents' home—a false, protected environment. When people were on vacation they didn't always act in character. Had she fallen in love with a man who did not really exist? On more than one occasion he'd seemed too good to be true.

Sandra came outside with George in her arms. "I can't understand why you have to go away this weekend, just when Cameron's coming home. He's bound to want to see you."

Radley zipped up his leather jacket and went to his mother. He kissed her cheek, then cupped George's head in his hand and pressed his lips to the baby's temple. "I need to get out in the fresh air, get some adrenaline pumping. I need a break from all this domestic stuff."

His mother sighed and patted his arm. "I guess we have rather taken over your life. But you've done wonderfully, hasn't he, Olivia?"

Olivia nodded numbly. Did Radley really need a break from her and George?

"You'd better take George inside. The wind's bitter," Radley said.

"You go carefully on that wretched machine." Sandra gave the motorcycle an evil glare, then rushed in the front door with George cuddled close.

Olivia wasn't happy about Radley riding the motorcycle either, but he insisted on leaving his car so she and Cameron could use it over the weekend.

Radley secured his bag to the back of his bike and turned. He wrapped her in his arms, hugging her so tightly she could barely breathe. "I miss you already," he whispered.

"Then don't go."

His lips thinned in a tight line. "It's for the best."

"Where exactly are you going?"

"Mum knows. It's a place in Wales where I've been climbing before."

Olivia didn't like the idea of him climbing there. It was bitterly cold and probably snowing in Wales. He might slip or get frostbite. She felt sick at the thought of him being in danger. She had no idea how she would cope when he was posted to another war zone.

At least he wasn't climbing on his own. He planned to meet another army doctor there. Someone called

Julia. Olivia wasn't over the moon about that either. Apparently Julia was a friend. That's all Radley had to say on the matter.

"I love you," Olivia said, hanging on to him when he tried to move away.

He hugged her tightly again and kissed her neck. "I love you too." He raised his head and gazed into her eyes. "I will be back soon. You need time with Cameron. I need to blow away the cobwebs and get some perspective on things."

"Okay."

Radley tensed to step back, so Olivia reluctantly let him go.

"Look after my nephew."

"I will." It troubled her that this was the first time Radley had referred to George that way. Had he distanced himself from her baby as well?

He pushed on his helmet and fastened the chin strap. Straddling his bike, he started the engine. It roared to life, effectively ruling out further conversation. This was it. He was going away.

He gunned the engine and the bike sped away, spitting gravel in its wake. Olivia wrapped her arms around her middle, shivering as the winter wind hummed in the trees.

It was Friday afternoon and Radley would be home on Monday. So why did she feel like she was losing him forever?

The sound of the front door banging echoed through the house and reached Olivia where she helped Sandra prepare dinner in the kitchen. Her heart leaped, hoping Radley had changed his mind and returned.

Both she and Sandra turned towards the door as a burst of music sounded, then abruptly cut off. "Hi," a male voice said. Cameron appeared in the doorway, his phone to his ear. "Yeah, I've just arrived." His gaze swept over them. He switched to German for another couple of sentences, then ended the call.

"Sorry about that." Cameron pocketed his phone.

Sandra rushed to hug him. "It's so good to see you. I've missed you, darling."

"You too, Mum." Cameron hugged her back.

"You've been away so long. I hope you've booked leave for Christmas."

"Yeah, I'll try to get home, Mum."

"You won't try. You'll be here. Where else would you want to go at Christmas?"

Cameron pulled a face that Olivia couldn't interpret.

Olivia examined the lanky young man she'd once known so well and felt...nothing. He was still good-looking with similar dark hair and eyes to Radley, yet she wasn't attracted to him anymore. The spark was gone.

"Hello, Cam," she said, folding her arms and leaning back on the kitchen counter. A few months ago she would have been angry with him for staying away so long. The anger had faded, but she certainly wasn't going to give him a welcoming embrace after he'd ignored her for months.

"Livi." Cameron's expression tensed, lines bracketing his mouth as though he were troubled. "I owe you an apology."

That wasn't what she'd expected him to say. It thawed her chilly attitude a little.

"Can we erase the last few months and start afresh?" Cameron's gaze moved to George, sitting in his seat on the table, where Olivia had put him so he could watch her and Sandra.

Wonder flickered across Cameron's face. The tightness inside Olivia softened some more.

"Meet George," she said.

"Your son," Sandra added in a pointed tone.

Cameron glanced at his mother, a sheepish smile on

his face.

Sandra put her hand on his shoulder and squeezed. "You've got a lot of catching up to do. Your little boy needs a father."

"Yeah, okay. Give me time to get used to the idea." Cameron walked across to the table.

Olivia moved to his side and ran a finger over George's tiny hand. "You can touch him. He won't break."

"Should I wash my hands first? I've been traveling for hours."

Olivia was surprised by Cameron's thoughtfulness. Careful hygiene must come from his medical training.

"Yes, good idea." Sandra set the water running, then stepped away from the sink.

With clean hands, Cameron touched his index finger to George's palm. A delighted smile lit his face when the baby's tiny fingers curled around his digit. Cameron shook hands with his son, his lips stretching into a grin. "Does that mean he likes me?"

"Yes, I think it does," Sandra said.

Cameron tickled George. He gurgled happily and his legs pedaled. "Can I hold him?"

A gamut of conflicting emotions raced through Olivia. It was obvious Cameron had taken to George, and her little boy seemed to like his father. This was great for George, she told herself as she tried to push memories of Radley holding the baby out of her mind.

"Unclip him." She watched while Cameron did as she suggested. "When you pick him up, make sure to support his head."

Cameron carefully lifted his son and cradled him on his chest. "Hey, bud, we're going to be pals, aren't we?"

The cold, hard nugget of resentment she'd built up against Cameron over the months when he'd ignored her softened some more. He wasn't the heartless monster she'd imagined him to be.

It took no time at all for Cameron to look at ease with George cradled in his arms. Then he didn't seem to want to put him down. He circled the room, rocking George, singing him nursery rhymes, and kissing his head.

"It's really kinda cool having a baby that looks like me." Cameron's gaze shifted from George and jumped between his mother and Olivia. "He does look like me, doesn't he?"

"Very much." Sandra pulled a picture of George out from under a fridge magnet and held it up beside a framed baby photo of Radley and Cameron on the kitchen dresser. "See. The three of you are like peas in a pod."

Cameron chuckled. "Just as well you didn't know Radley nine months ago or I'd be worried he might be George's dad."

The breath caught in Olivia's chest, burning with a mix of emotions that threatened to overwhelm her. If only she had known Radley back then, if only he were George's father. A burst of guilt followed that thought and she turned away, unable to watch Cameron with her baby any longer.

She could not change the facts. Somehow they would all have to deal with this and learn to live with the situation. She wanted whatever was best for her darling little boy, but she desperately hoped the outcome did not hurt Radley.

Radley dug his chilled fingers in a rocky nook and hauled himself up another foot on the rough granite rock face, wedging the toe of his shoe on a ledge. Tiny specks of snow in the bitter wind stung his exposed skin. He was starting to think that climbing in Wales in the middle of winter hadn't been such a good plan.

"You're mental, Knight," Major Julia Braithwaite shouted from a few feet below him. "Next time you call for a climbing partner, remind me to tell you to get lost."

Radley pushed a nut into a crevice, checked it was firm, then snapped a carabiner on the wire to secure his rope. A wry smile pulled at his chapped lips. Doctors needed to be able to laugh in the face of unbearable conditions, army doctors especially, and he could always count on Julia to entertain him.

In Afghanistan, Julia had kept them all amused with her crazy antics and bawdy stories. She gave the impression that she didn't care about anything, but she was the most reliable anesthetist he'd ever worked with.

Another couple of minutes passed while Radley scrambled up the sheer granite cliff in the freezing winter weather. Despite the difficult conditions and Julia's banter, visions of Olivia and George played continuously through Radley's thoughts—Olivia wrapped in his arms, warm and sleepy in bed; George splashing his little legs in his warm bath.

Radley sat back in his harness to wipe his numb face on his sleeve. He missed them so much it was killing him.

"Get your ass moving, Knight. I'm freezing my goolies off down here." Once again Julia's voice stirred him into action. He took the last few steps that brought his fingers to the top of the cliff, found a handhold, and heaved himself up on the rocky ledge.

He steadied the rope joining him to Julia as she followed him up. She slumped down on her backside, wiping a gloved hand over her mouth. "If the snow is too bad for the helicopter to make it up here and we have to climb down, I'm going to roast your ass, Knight."

She punched him in the arm and he winced. She might be small, but she packed a mean bunch of fives.

Radley pulled out his phone and dialed the local

airport where his contact was waiting. "We'll be ready in ten. Just got to walk to the pickup zone."

"Okay, mate. You're cutting it close. We should just get you down before we're grounded by bad weather."

"What did he say?" Julia demanded.

"We've got to climb down." Radley spoiled his joke because he couldn't keep a straight face.

"Funny, Knight. Real funny."

She stood and gathered up the kit. Radley joined her and they set out to slog their way to the large flat area a short distance to the east.

The regular *whump whump whump* of the helicopter blades was a welcome sound. A few minutes later, they were inside the chopper out of the bitter wind.

Julia chatted with the pilot, but Radley stared out the window at the bleak, high moorland and craggy rocks of the Black Mountains, now dotted with patches of snow.

It would be so easy to get into trouble up here. He shouldn't have come climbing in these conditions. It was crazy dangerous. All the things Julia had said and more. What was he trying to prove? He didn't even know.

All he did know was that he wanted to be safely back with Olivia and George so she wouldn't worry about him.

The aircraft swooped low over Abergavenny and landed in a field belonging to Julia's husband. The two of them jumped out and crouched to run clear of the chopper blades.

A pickup was parked in the gateway. Julia jumped in beside her husband and Radley climbed in the back.

He pulled off his gloves and protective headgear and ran fingers through his hair. To hell with staying away until Monday—one night had been enough. He wanted to hold Olivia in his arms and hug George. It was a ten-minute drive to the Braithwaites's farm. Then fifteen minutes to pack his bag and load up his bike. He could be on the road heading home in half an hour. That would get him to his parents' place by dinnertime.

He was done with giving Cameron space to win Olivia back. If Cameron wanted her, he would have to fight Radley for her.

Radley pulled out his phone and scrolled through his contacts. He was about to call Olivia when the device chimed. With an irritated frown, he put it to his ear.

"Knight, here."

His teeth clenched as he was issued orders for immediate deployment to Afghanistan. No reason was given, but he knew something serious must have taken place for this to happen.

Radley cut the call and dropped his head back against the seat. This screwed up his plans. Now Olivia would think he'd run out on her.

Chapter Six

Lights strobed and music throbbed. The combination was fast giving Olivia a headache. She had never much liked nightclubs. Right now this was the last place she wanted to be, but Cameron had insisted they come out to celebrate the end of her exams.

The hot, bustling space filled with giggling girls and posturing men seemed to suit Cameron. He stood chatting animatedly with a group of his friends. He'd said they were *their* friends when he talked her into coming out. But not one of them had bothered to visit her in the hospital or help her when she'd been desperate.

She had nothing in common with these people—girls with barely anything on and men swaggering around with huge egos.

While she'd been Cameron's girlfriend, this had been their normal weekend socializing. Olivia had grown out of this. It seemed Cameron had not.

She sidled through the throng of scantily clad women all holding cocktails, and leaned in to put her mouth to Cameron's ear. "I want to go home."

"Already?" He said something else, but she couldn't hear him over the pounding music.

"I'll need to feed George soon," she shouted in his ear.

"My mother will do that." Cameron chugged down the rest of his pint of beer and held up his glass. "Whose round is it?" Someone passed him another full glass.

He'd already downed three pints. A few more and he'd be falling over drunk. He turned away and started talking to a group of friends again. She pulled on his sleeve so hard his new pint of beer sloshed on the floor.

"Be careful," he said.

"I want to go home. Now." Olivia tapped her watch for emphasis.

Someone spoke to Cameron and his attention moved off her again. He'd had so much to drink he couldn't concentrate. She was wasting her time. She hadn't wanted to come here. If only she had stuck to her guns and not let him talk her into it. Sandra hadn't helped. She'd encouraged Olivia to go out and enjoy herself. But she probably had no idea what a dive this place was.

Holding her purse tightly against her chest, she angled her body and pushed through the crowd towards the exit. The stink of alcohol, sweat, and mingled perfume filled her nose. Spatters of drink splashed her arm, or at least she hoped the liquid was drink. She elbowed and shoved to get free. Eventually she burst out of the stifling atmosphere into the crisp, clear winter night.

Olivia snatched a breath of clean air and let it out on a sigh of relief, even though the chill made her shiver. That was the last time she ever went inside a place like that.

A group of men who were obviously drunk shouted obscene suggestions to her. Feeling vulnerable and alone, she crossed the road to pass them and hurried towards the taxi line. With a burst of relief she climbed into a cab and gave the address. Very aware it wasn't safe to be traveling on her own late at night, she pulled out her mobile phone to call Sandra. "I'm in a taxi heading home. I should only be fifteen minutes." She made sure she spoke loud enough that the cab driver heard the conversation.

She asked about George, then ended the call and wrapped her arms around herself, trying to warm up. This was not the way she'd imagined celebrating the end of her exams. She'd much rather have spent the evening with Radley in the Hunter's Moon, eating a nice meal while looking out over the moonlit canal.

If Radley were here, he'd never have let her go home alone. He'd have watched the clock, ready to leave in plenty of time to get back for George's feed. He'd be sitting next to her, his arm around her shoulders to keep her warm on the chilly winter night.

Cameron might like the novelty of having a son, but it had taken only twenty-four hours before he put his own pleasure before his son's care.

The taxi drove up the drive and stopped outside Willow House. Olivia paid and jumped out, desperately pleased to be back at the place that felt like a sanctuary from the world, even though it was only a temporary home.

She let herself in the front door and ran upstairs to the bedroom. Sandra was sitting on her bed when she entered, George lying quietly at her side, his diaper clean, all ready to feed before he went back to sleep.

Even in the low light, one look at Sandra told Olivia something was wrong. A flash of foreboding raced through her, followed by a real sense of fear. "What's happened?"

"Radley called."

Olivia's fist clenched over her heart. "He's fallen and hurt himself?"

"No, no." Sandra seemed to rouse from her depressed mood and placed a steadying hand on Olivia's elbow. "Radley's fine. But he's been sent back

61

to Afghanistan."

"Afghanistan?"

At Sandra's nod, Olivia frowned in confusion. "He's only just come back from there. He's on leave."

"He's not on leave anymore. The army can cancel leave whenever it suits them. I know." She laughed without humor. "I've lived with this my whole married life. The army comes first."

"But Radley was climbing in Wales." Olivia still couldn't wrap her head around the situation.

Sandra glanced at the clock. "He'll be over the Atlantic by now. He was headed to RAF Brize Norton when he called. They were flying him straight out to perform emergency surgery on a medical technician. That's all he was able to tell me."

Olivia sat down on the bed with a bump, her heart pounding. She'd read up on the work of the army medical corps. It sounded as though they were rarely injured, but there was always a risk.

"I'm frightened he'll be hurt."

"That's what you have to live with if you're an army wife," Sandra said.

"Why did they send Radley? He's only just come back after nine months. Don't they have other doctors out there?"

"Radley is a specialist at limb-salvage surgery after severe trauma. If they needed him, it'll be serious."

Olivia picked up her little boy and held him close, burying her nose in his fine, dark hair, taking comfort from his familiar smell. Radley was gone, shipped out to Afghanistan without a chance to say good-bye.

He did an important job, she knew that. But she had lived her life never knowing when her father would come home, watching her mother struggling on her own. He'd been in the merchant navy, not the forces, but it came to the same thing—an absent father. She wanted George to have a father figure in his life who was there for him. She wanted the man she loved by her side.

Someone shook Radley's shoulder. He woke as the RAF Hercules aircraft touched down at Camp Bastion. He'd slept nearly the whole flight from RAF Brize Norton in the UK to Kandahar in Afghanistan, where he switched aircrafts to fly on to the main operating base.

In his years in the army, he'd learned to nap wherever and whenever he could. He certainly needed it. After his strenuous day's climbing in Wales, he'd been traveling all night.

He'd been supplied with a uniform, and he'd donned body armor and a helmet when they entered Afghan airspace. He grabbed his bag and headed to the exit. A corporal was waiting for him as he stepped off the plane. The man saluted. "If you'll come with me, sir. They're ready for you."

He'd had a brief chat with his father on the phone while he'd waited to board his plane. He knew he'd be going straight into the operating room to work on a serious casualty that needed his specialist skills.

The jeep bumped over debris from a recent attack on the base, one that hadn't made the news before he left the UK. His mother and Olivia would be worried when they heard.

Radley grabbed the window frame to steady himself as he gazed out at the familiar bleak, sandy landscape. The wind whipped up mini dust tornados and he tasted grit. He'd thought the rugged Welsh hill country was bleak in winter, and it was, but in a majestic, awe-inspiring way. The endless sand, dust, and sticky humid conditions here were bleak in another way altogether.

The place sucked at his spirit as if it would drain the energy and enthusiasm for life right out of him. But even here, so far away from England, the memory of being with Olivia and George made him smile, giving him a reason to live that he'd not known he was missing before.

The familiar sight of the hospital came into view. Radley straightened, rubbed a hand over his face, and composed himself. This was the busiest NATO hospital in Afghanistan, fitted out with everything the medical team needed to offer emergency treatment to wounded military personnel and local people.

The jeep stopped and Radley jumped out.

"Radley. Major Knight." His father's booming voice had Radley standing to attention.

He saluted formally, then moved forward to shake his father's hand. "Where do you want me?"

"Have you slept?"

"On the plane."

"Excellent." His father nodded as they entered the building, medical personnel jumping out of the way as Brigadier Knight approached. "This might be a long stint. We have three seriously injured in the recent attack; two have already been in the OR. One is now being prepped to fly back to the military hospital at home. We need to stabilize the other before he can go. Unfortunately we haven't been able to do much for the third, Sergeant Kent. He's a medical technician and he's going to lose his arm unless you can save it."

The last trace of Radley's weariness fell away as he focused. Determination ran along his nerves. He donned scrubs and washed up. A nurse helped him into his gown and gloves, then he entered the OR.

A prayer whispered through his mind as he nodded to the medical team who would work with him, noticing some familiar faces and acknowledging a few of them by name. "Good morning, I'm Major Knight," he said as he approached the table and scanned the patient.

He made eye contact with the anesthetist. "Ready?"

"Yes, sir."

She was a captain like Cameron, a young doctor probably on her first tour of duty. But she must have proved she could cope or she wouldn't be here.

"Good." Radley indicated where he wanted the lights positioned, donned his surgical eye loupes that gave him a magnified view of the injury, and moved in to examine the arm of the man on the table. The limb was severely compromised, the blast damage so serious any normal surgeon wouldn't even try to save it.

Radley had started as an orthopedic surgeon, then worked on a special microsurgery program to deal with just this sort of injury. He was one of only a handful of doctors who could save this man's arm.

This was why he'd practiced so hard to master his skills, to help men like Sergeant Kent. For the first time since his leave had been canceled, he was glad they'd called him back.

"Leave canceled. Sorry. Talk to you when I can. Love, Rad."

Olivia stared at the screen of her phone, rereading the text from Radley for the hundredth time. He must have sent it before he left the UK, yet she hadn't received it until Sunday morning. At least he had thought of her in his rush to leave.

George whimpered in her arms. Olivia moved him over to her other breast and continued to feed.

"How are you doing?" Sandra asked, coming through the sitting room door with a cup of coffee in her hand.

Olivia tucked away her phone and smiled. "Okay, I guess."

Sandra set down the hot drink and dropped into a chair with a sigh. "I'm sorry about last night. I can't believe Cameron let you come home alone, and then later..." Her voice trailed off and she shook her head. "I thought he'd grown up."

Olivia's thoughts went back to the early hours of the morning when Cameron had finally made his way home. A noise had woken her about four a.m. The sound of something crashing downstairs had brought her from her bed.

Staggering around the entrance hall, Cameron had knocked a vase of flowers off a table. Sandra joined her at the top of the stairs, tying the cord on a pink dressing gown.

"Bathroom," Cameron slurred, his hand covering his mouth.

Olivia and Sandra dashed downstairs and guided him to the toilet where he threw up.

"Oh, Cameron," Sandra said, her tone full of exasperation.

Olivia stood aside while Cameron's mother wet a washcloth and cleaned him up as if he were a child.

This was the father of her baby. What a brilliant example he would be to George.

"I'm so sorry you had to see this." Poor Sandra looked mortified as she and Olivia helped Cameron out of the bathroom. There was no way they could get him upstairs in this state, so Sandra grabbed some old towels and spread them on the floor in the small nook where they watched TV and listened to music. They lowered him down. He immediately zonked out.

Ten hours later he was still asleep.

Sandra glanced in the direction of the nook with a worried look. "I'll have to wake him soon or he'll miss his flight back to Germany."

"So much for him spending time with George." Cameron had wasted Sunday, sleeping off his night of indulgence, instead of using this precious time to get to know his son. Olivia pressed her lips to her baby's head to ease the little pang of hurt she felt on his behalf.

Olivia's phone chimed. She grabbed it out of her

pocket and stared at the screen.

"I love you." That was all the text from Radley said. It was enough to send her heart soaring and bring a happy smile to her lips. For a moment she forgot where she was, and once again she was snuggled in his arms in her bed, the sound of his heartbeat beneath her ear.

"Radley?" Sandra asked, jolting Olivia back to reality.

She nodded.

"He must have landed safely," Sandra continued, a thoughtful expression on her face. "You love him, don't you?"

"Yes." Relief washed through Olivia at being able to admit her feelings.

"And he loves you?"

Olivia held up her phone so Sandra could see the message Radley had sent.

"I prayed this might happen." A smile flickered over Sandra's face, then faded. "I was losing hope that Cameron would do his duty by you, so I threw you and Radley together and crossed my fingers."

She heaved a sigh and scraped back her hair. "I'm sorry. Cameron's behaving like an adolescent, and Radley's wedded to the damn army like his father. I shouldn't have interfered, but you're such a pretty girl. I was sure as soon as you started work, some wealthy lawyer would snap you up. Then I'd lose you and the little one."

Sandra rested a tender hand on George's back as Olivia burped him. "I was selfish. I couldn't bear the thought I might lose my grandson."

"I'd never stop you seeing him."

"I know you wouldn't. But if you married another man, it's only natural that he'd be George's father, and his parents would become George's grandparents. I don't want some peripheral role in his life. I want to be his nana."

So Sandra had purposely thrown her and Radley together. She'd probably watched their relationship develop. Olivia wasn't sure how she felt about being manipulated. She bit her lip in thought. She supposed that it didn't matter how she and Radley had gotten together. What mattered is they had, and she loved him.

"It's okay."

"It's not, though." Sandra cast a troubled glance at the door as footsteps sounded. "Now Cameron's come home and confused matters."

Cameron appeared in the doorway, a sheepish grin on his face. "One hell of a celebration last night, Liv."

There was so much Olivia wanted to say that the words tumbled around in her head and jammed in her mouth. She could spout a tirade of criticism and complaint or say nothing. She clenched her jaw and chose to remain silent. What was the point in yelling at him? He would leave for his flight soon. She probably wouldn't see him again for months.

"Can I have something to eat, Mum?" Cameron checked the time on his phone as he wandered closer. "A mate is picking me up in thirty minutes."

Sandra rushed off to the kitchen. Cameron flopped down in the chair she'd vacated. He leaned forward and touched the back of George's head. Olivia hoped he'd washed his hands. The faint odor of vomit still hung around him, and he had specks of it on his clothes.

"Can I hold him?" Cameron asked. "It's my last chance before I go."

Olivia bit back a comment about all the wasted hours he'd slept that day.

"Shower and change your clothes." Olivia pointed at the dirty marks. "You can hold him when you're clean."

Cameron picked at the stains, his nose wrinkled. "I will in a sec. I thought you'd want to talk about George first."

She'd planned to discuss lots of things with Cameron, one of the main ones being finance. She was really tight for money because she hadn't been able to work. Her meager savings had gone for baby equipment. But as she stared at this young man who still behaved like an irresponsible student, she decided she'd rather face the future alone than depend on him for anything. Anyway, she hoped she and George had a future with Radley.

"I have nothing I want to say."

"I do." Cameron sat up and rubbed a hand over his mouth. "I'm sorry I didn't contact you sooner. I do want to be part of George's life. Let me help pay for his keep."

"Keep? He's not a pet."

He gestured in irritation. "I'm trying to be reasonable here, Liv. Don't make this difficult."

"No." She shook her head and held her darling little boy closer. "I don't need you to pay anything."

Cameron's expression tightened. "Then why have you been hassling me for months to contact you?"

"Because I wanted George to have his daddy in his life." She paused. "And I did need help," she added reluctantly. "Luckily your mum has been wonderful."

"I expect she's paid for half this stuff." Cameron waved his arm around, indicating the stroller parked in the corner and the other baby things. "I'd better pay her back."

Heat rushed into Olivia's cheeks. She really wanted to tell him not to, but she had no right to expect Sandra to keep putting her hand in her pocket. Even though she said she didn't mind.

What would Radley make of this? Should she tell Cameron that she and Radley were together? Except right now they weren't. Radley was halfway around the world in some godforsaken place, and she had no idea when she'd see him again. He'd said he loved her, but he'd made her no promises.

"If you can afford it, I'm sure your mum would appreciate the gesture. I promised to pay her back, but it will be awhile before I'm able to."

"Okay, that's settled. I'll send you some money each month for George." Cameron jumped up and headed to the door. "I'll have a quick shower and be back for my good-bye hug with my boy."

Olivia stared at the door long after Cameron had disappeared. *His boy.* If Cameron was determined to accept his role as George's dad, where would Radley fit into her son's life?

Chapter Seven

Olivia parked Radley's car in the town's main square and climbed out. A tall Christmas tree stood in the town center, decorated with colored lights while cheery holiday tunes sounded from the nearby stores.

She couldn't believe it was only ten days until Christmas. George was nearly three months old. That meant she'd known Radley for that length of time. For six weeks of it they'd been together virtually 24/7. Then he'd gone back to Afghanistan and left her unsure what the future held for them. Or if there was a *them* at all.

Fear and foreboding pulsed in a hollow place in her chest, as it always did when she thought of Radley now. She hated that he was in a war zone, at risk of being hurt. She missed him so much yet he'd only called her once since he left.

It wasn't Radley's fault his leave had been canceled, but she hadn't had a chance to say a proper good-bye. She couldn't help feeling abandoned. Sandra said it was difficult for the troops to call from Afghanistan. That did sound likely, yet Cameron now Skyped once a week from Germany so he could see his son.

Radley had access to a computer because he'd e-mailed, so why couldn't he Skype her as well? She would love to see his face. Wasn't he interested in seeing how George was changing, or in talking to her?

In his e-mails he just chatted about trivial things. He hadn't asked about the weekend Cameron came home, even after she mentioned that Cameron was now giving her money for George.

Radley said he loved her, yet it was meaningless if she never saw him. Her father still tossed out "I love you" when he called her, but he didn't or he would make the effort to see her occasionally.

Glancing at her watch, she hurried towards the realtor's office. She'd started doing a couple of shifts a week at an old people's residential home, a similar job to one she'd done in the past to supplement her student loan. Her shift began in twenty minutes, so she had to be quick.

Christmas lights hung from the street lamps and spanned the road, lighting up the area as darkness fell. Olivia paused outside a toy store to examine the display of cuddly animals. She hadn't bought any presents yet. At least now she had some earnings she could purchase small gifts for the Knights and George.

A few moments later, she pushed open the glass door to the realtor's office and glanced around. The woman who had met her and Radley at Brook View Cottage was seated near the back. Olivia approached and smiled, noting the woman's name on her desk.

"Hello, Lindsey, I need to talk to you about Brook View Cottage. The one Radley Knight is buying."

Lindsey looked up, recognition in her eyes. "Of course. How can I help? I hope there isn't a problem with the purchase."

"Not a problem, just a delay."

Olivia explained that the contract had arrived but Radley couldn't sign yet as he was in Afghanistan. Sandra had called the lawyers' office but they refused to discuss the transaction with her because of the Data Protection Act. They would only talk to Radley and that was obviously impossible right now. Olivia hoped the realtor might be more helpful.

"Is it possible for you to contact the seller to explain why there's a delay? We don't want him to think that Radley's lost interest."

"Shouldn't be a problem. Sit down for a moment. I'll call him now."

Olivia sat and laced her fingers together over her tummy, still aware of the tenderness over the C-section scar. A small silver Christmas tree adorned a filing cabinet, and glittery baubles hung from the ceiling. Signs of Christmas were everywhere, yet Olivia had never felt less like celebrating. The only good thing about Christmas was that by the time it arrived, she would have her exam results.

When the realtor's call was answered, Olivia listened carefully to the side of the conversation she could hear. It didn't seem to be going well. Lines appeared on the young woman's forehead and she apologized a few times.

When she put down the phone, she sighed. "It's not good news, I'm afraid. Mr. Knight promised the sale would be completed by Christmas. The seller is depending on that. He needs the money for his own purchase."

"It's not Radley's fault. His leave was canceled unexpectedly. He was recalled to Afghanistan."

The woman nodded. "My cousin's in the army, so I sympathize. The trouble is there's another couple interested in Brook View who offered cash. The seller says if they can rush through the deal before Christmas, he'll sell to them instead. I'm sorry."

Olivia gasped as though she had been punched in the chest. Radley had set his heart on Brook View and she loved it too. This was so unfair. Everything was going wrong.

She pressed her lips together and nodded. "Thank you for finding out for me. At least we know."

Olivia trudged out into the bitter evening air. She felt so helpless and frustrated. If only she or Sandra could act on Radley's behalf, the cottage would be his. If she stayed with Radley, would it always be like this—him away, her struggling to deal with things on her own?

She'd managed alone ever since her mother died. But now she had George. She really didn't want to handle everything alone. George should have a proper family with a mum and dad both there to care for him, the sort of life she had missed out on as a child. She wanted the man she loved by her side, sharing things. Not halfway around the world.

It was just after midnight when Olivia let herself quietly into Willow House after a shift at work, and headed for the stairs. The sound of a sob from the sitting room pulled her up. She frowned for a moment before changing direction.

She pushed open the sitting room door to reveal the softly lit room. The log fire had died down. In the glowing light from the embers, Sandra kneeled beside a Christmas tree that hadn't been there when Olivia left.

The tree was partially decorated, the mini lights in place and some shiny balls on the lower branches. As Olivia moved closer, she saw boxes of decorations on the floor.

Sandra was rocking George in her arms. It was only as Olivia reached her side that she realized the sob hadn't come from the baby. Radley's mother was crying.

A shock of fear raced through her. She crouched beside the older woman. "What's wrong?"

"Oh, nothing, just me being silly." Sandra wiped her cheeks with the back of a hand. "My husband was meant to call tonight. I've been waiting for hours, watching the clock, but no call." She gave a hollow laugh. "After all this time, I know it doesn't mean anything. I must be hormonal or something. Maybe I'm missing him more than usual because I was decorating the tree."

Olivia pulled over a footstool and sat at Sandra's side. After being on her feet for so many hours, she needed to sit down. Sandra passed George across to her and he nuzzled her shirtfront. "Are you hungry, little man? Just for a change."

Sandra gave a watery laugh and stroked George's hair. "He's such a good boy. He reminds me so much of Radley."

"Not Cameron?" Olivia said in surprise. After all, Cameron was the dad.

"Lord, no. Cameron was a handful, very noisy and very demanding. He needed to be constantly entertained. Radley was happy with his own company like George."

"I'm sorry Brigadier Knight didn't call," Olivia said. "I suppose he's too busy or not near a phone."

Sandra sighed deeply and rose to her feet. "You're right. I'm sure." She stooped and gathered up some baubles, then hung them on the tree. "I hoped he'd be home for Christmas, but last time we spoke, he didn't know. With the current troubles, there's a strong possibility it will be just you, me, and little George for Christmas this year."

She wiped away another tear and added more baubles to the branches. Her melancholy mood was catching. Olivia's own worries about Radley welled up and her eyes filled. She swallowed back the need to cry. "Aren't you used to this?"

"Gosh, yes. When we first married, my husband was only a captain. He had no say if he got home for Christmas. But in those days the boys were little, and Christmas is so much about children. We lived in army married quarters, and the holiday season was filled with events for the kids. Then just before Christmas I'd bundle up the two boys and drive down to my parents' house in Hampshire. They had a beautiful place in the New Forest."

"That sounds nice." Olivia remembered her childhood Christmases, just her and her mum, her dad rarely making the effort to come home from wherever in the world he was working. But he hadn't been kept away by orders, only by his indifference.

"I thought the time apart would get easier as the years went on, but with the boys gone too..." Sandra's words trailed away, and she cleared her throat.

"A brigadier can normally choose when he takes leave, but with the recent flare-up of hostilities in Afghanistan, I don't know if he'll make it back. He has a strong sense of duty and Radley takes after his father. This might be the first year ever that I don't have any of them home."

"Well, you have us," Olivia said.

"Yes. Thank heaven for you two." Sandra stopped and folded her arms around Olivia and her baby, hugging them tight. "You don't know how pleased I am to have you here, love. Don't ever think you're imposing. You're not. You and this little darling are a godsend to me."

The tears flooded back in Olivia's eyes at Sandra's heartfelt words. She had been planning to move out after Christmas, had already started looking for an apartment. Since her mother died, she had been alone. Her father occasionally contacted her, but she was lucky to see him once a year.

"I'm glad we'll be here with you for Christmas. I'm looking forward to it." And for the first time, she realized she was. This had been a tough year. She had faced challenges she had never dreamed of. Now she had her darling little boy. He was the best thing that had ever happened to her.

Sandra took Olivia's hand and squeezed it. "I hope Radley marries you and makes sure you stay in the family."

"If the army ever lets him come home." Olivia stared pensively into the dying fire, all her uncertainties flooding back.

"At least you've had a taste of what it's like to be an army wife before you take the plunge. You have to love a man very much to put up with always coming in second to his career."

While he waited to retrieve his baggage, Radley's finger hovered over the screen of his phone. He longed to send Olivia a text saying, "Back in the UK!" With a sigh, he resisted, and dropped the device back in his pocket. It was unfair to raise her hopes that he would be home for Christmas when he wasn't absolutely sure he'd make it.

"There you go," his father said, pointing at the luggage carousel at RAF Brize Norton in baggage claim. "That's yours, isn't it?"

Radley grabbed his bag while his father picked up his own. They headed out through the bustle of arrivals and departures where forces personnel mingled together with a few civilian family members.

They left the main terminal building and a corporal met them at the door and saluted. "I have your car, sir," he said to Radley's father. He led them to a black limo and stowed their luggage in the trunk.

Radley climbed in the back of the vehicle beside his father. Nepotism was alive and well in the British army and Radley was thankful for it. Otherwise he'd be on a bus heading for the train station to find his own way to London.

Once they were moving, Radley pulled off his cap and ran his fingers through his gritty hair. He was looking forward to a luxury hotel room with a soft bed and a shower. His father opened his briefcase and started perusing official documents. Radley sighed and pulled out his phone again to check his e-mails, hoping there might be one from Olivia.

"Have you told Mum you'll be home for Christmas?" he asked his father.

"Not yet." The brigadier didn't look up from his work.

"It's only three days away. She'll be wondering."

Finally his father raised his gaze. "I'm almost certain we'll both be there, but I don't want to say anything, just in case. There's nothing worse than letting the women down. It's much better to keep quiet, then it's a pleasant surprise when we turn up."

"Or you hope it's pleasant," Radley said.

His father laughed. "Very true."

Radley tapped the screen of his phone. He couldn't resist texting something to Olivia. He satisfied himself by sending the same thing he'd sent many times before. "I love you. R." Although after nearly six weeks with little contact, she was probably growing weary of proclamations of love with nothing to back them up.

He scrolled to his photos and went through the ones he had snapped of George and Olivia. He realized now that he'd taken the special time with them for granted. His spell of playing happy family had ended unexpectedly. He wanted that life for real, but it sounded as though Cameron had now staked his claim on George. Radley had no idea how things would pan out when he arrived home.

The colors of the English countryside whizzed past the window as the car sped down the motorway, such a welcome change from the sepia tones of the desert. He dozed for a while and woke as they entered central London. The car dropped them at a discreet hotel in Whitehall. He quickly showered and changed into service dress before meeting his father back in the lobby.

The car picked them up again and transported them to the huge gray edifice that housed the Ministry of Defense. They entered the tall doors and passed through security, then rode the elevator to the correct floor.

His father saluted a superior officer, which was something Radley didn't see very often, and they stopped outside a suite of offices.

"George, good to see you." Lieutenant General Platt, one of Radley's father's oldest friends, met them at the door. He shook hands with Brigadier Knight and they disappeared into the office, leaving Radley to wait outside.

"Would you like a cup of tea or coffee, sir," a young woman in uniform asked him.

"Yes, coffee. Cream, no sugar. Thank you."

She brought his drink, then returned to her desk and started tapping at her computer keyboard.

Radley picked up a magazine and flipped through it halfheartedly. His father was here to discuss a potential move to work for the Ministry of Defense, but Radley had no idea why he'd been ordered to attend.

A little over an hour later, his father came to the door and beckoned him inside. The three-star general indicated Radley should take the vacant chair in front of his desk. His father regained his seat to the side and picked up a half-finished glass of whisky.

"Well, Major Knight. The first order of business is to congratulate your father on his new appointment with the Ministry of Defense." The two older men shared a look. "And his promotion to major general, but please keep that under your hat for a few weeks until it's officially announced."

"Congratulations, sir." Radley beamed at his father, thinking how pleased his mum would be to have his dad based in London for the foreseeable future.

Lieutenant General Platt poured a finger of whisky in another glass and handed it to Radley. Then he raised his glass towards Radley's father. "To Queen and country," he said, "and your continued success in their defense."

They all knocked back the contents of their tumblers and the double malt burned its way down Radley's throat, spreading fire along his veins. Ever since his father told him they were coming here together, he'd been curious as to why they wanted to see him in the lofty halls of the MOD.

"I expect you're wondering why you're here, Major?" the senior officer said, as if reading his mind.

"Yes, sir."

"You might think we don't notice what goes on in field hospitals, but we do. I don't pretend to know anything about surgery, but I'm reliably informed you have a particular skill in dealing with acute trauma to limbs."

"Yes, sir," Radley repeated, wondering to which far-flung part of the world they would send him next, and silently praying he could take his remaining leave first and spend Christmas at home with Olivia and George before he left.

The lieutenant general smiled and opened a folder. "Well, Major Knight. I believe your next posting will interest you very much."

Chapter Eight

Olivia danced around the entrance hall of Willow House with George in her arms. Her exam results had arrived in the mail that day while she was at work, and she'd just opened the letter. She'd earned a first class honors degree! She couldn't wait to tell Sandra and Radley.

Excitement raced through her. Her hard work had paid off. Although her pleasure dimmed at the memory of the less-than-enthusiastic response she'd had when she contacted the local law firms to ask about training positions. It seemed all the vacancies had been taken by graduates who passed their exams in the summer.

But there would be other chances, she was sure of it, especially as she had done so well. She'd just have to persevere.

Sandra had looked after George for most of the day and slipped out for takeout when Olivia arrived home. Now the front door opened and Sandra came back with cartons of Chinese.

"I got a first," Olivia said, flapping the letter.

"You clever girl. What a wonderful Christmas present." Sandra grinned and gave her a hug. Then she kissed George's head. "This little chap is sure to be brainy having you and Cameron for parents."

Olivia's joy dimmed some more at the reminder of

Cameron. She wanted him in George's life, but he was being a pain. He'd asked his new girlfriend Kelly, who'd been a pediatric nurse, to e-mail Olivia advice on baby care. The woman was probably trying to be helpful, but it was very annoying to be told what to do by Cameron's girlfriend.

"Let's have dinner. I'm starving." Sandra led the way through to the kitchen where Olivia had already laid the table. "I'd suggest cracking open a bottle of wine to celebrate, but you can't drink as you're still breast-feeding, and I don't want to indulge alone."

"Go on, you deserve a glass." Olivia smiled with encouragement. She felt sorry for Sandra. There were only a few hours left of Christmas Eve and she still hadn't heard from Brigadier Knight. She'd more or less given up hope that he'd be home for Christmas Day.

Olivia felt the same way, although she tried to be positive. Radley had texted her his love the previous day, but she'd received so many similar texts from him that they didn't give her the boost they used to.

Olivia strapped George into the removable seat section of his stroller and set it on the table so he could watch them. "Are you a good boy?" She squeaked his soft Santa toy hanging on his seat. He smiled and waved his arms, babbling baby language.

They sat and started eating. "Any news on what's going on in Afghanistan?" Olivia asked.

"There's nothing new in the newspapers or on the Internet." Sandra tapped the screen of her tablet device and turned it so Olivia could see. "I searched earlier but all the relevant news is a week or two old."

"If things have quieted down out there, does that mean it's more likely the men will get leave?"

"One would think so, but over the years I've found it doesn't always work that way."

"Oh." Olivia's hopes had risen every day that passed without reports of trouble, yet the men still hadn't turned up. She glanced at the wall clock, draped with sparkly tinsel. A sigh rushed out between her lips. They were running out of time to make it home for tomorrow.

A noise sounded from the front hall. Olivia's gaze flew to the kitchen door.

"Someone's here." Sandra jumped up.

"Please, God, let it be Radley," Olivia said under her breath.

Cameron stepped through the door and her heart crashed down with disappointment. She immediately felt guilty for her reaction.

"Oh, darling." Sandra threw her arms around her younger son. "I'm so pleased to see you. Why didn't you let me know you were coming?"

"I did. I texted yesterday."

"Well, I didn't get it. I've been checking my phone umpteen times a day." She stood back, gripping his arms, and looked at him. "Anyway, it doesn't matter. I'm just pleased you're home."

"I couldn't miss my boy's first Christmas." Cameron's gaze moved to George and a grin pulled at the corners of his mouth. "How is the little guy?" He rounded the table and stopped to hug Olivia and kiss her cheek.

The meeting wasn't quite as awkward as last time he was home. They had gotten to know each other again through their video calls and communication about George. Cameron might have his faults, but there was no doubt he cared for his son.

Cameron pulled a soft toy dog wearing a Santa hat out of a bag and tickled George's tummy with it. The baby gurgled and kicked his legs. "You like that, don't you? You'll get more presents tomorrow." He fluffed up George's hair affectionately. "Can I take him out of his seat?"

"Of course."

"Put his other presents under the tree," Sandra added. "He's already been given a heap. Georgie's not going to know what's happened when he gets all his new toys tomorrow."

Olivia smiled as Cameron unclipped the straps and lifted his son into his arms. George held his head up and stared at his father for a while before the effort grew too much for his neck. He head-butted Cameron's shoulder. "Ouch." Cameron laughed. "Easy, Georgie, you'll knock yourself out."

Sandra set a third place at the table, then Cameron returned George to his seat and sat down to eat. Sandra beamed at him. Olivia was pleased for her—at least she had one of her sons home for Christmas.

The Chinese easily stretched to feed three as the portions were always generous. After they finished eating, Olivia cleared away the dishes and cartons and put on the coffee machine.

They were listening to Cameron tell stories about his work in Germany, when the sound of the front door opening cut through the conversation. For the second time that evening, Sandra leaped to her feet. The deep timbre of male voices set Olivia's heart racing—Radley, please let it be him.

Brigadier Knight filled the doorway with his imposing figure. Sandra flew into his arms and buried her face against his chest. He looked slightly bemused as he wrapped her in his embrace.

"You made it back for Christmas," she gasped tearfully.

"You knew I'd try."

Her answer was half laugh, half sob.

Radley followed his father in. Sandra released her husband and pulled her older son into a hug. "You're thoughtless, both of you. Neither of you told me you were coming."

"We weren't sure until yesterday evening. Then we

84

decided to make it a surprise," Radley said. "It's good to be back."

"All my boys are home. I can't believe it. A few hours ago I thought Olivia and I would be celebrating Christmas on our own."

Radley's gaze rose from his mother to find Olivia. Her heart pounded, her limbs suddenly weak. She longed to throw herself in his arms, but it wouldn't be appropriate. Brigadier Knight and Cameron didn't know about her relationship with Radley yet.

The brigadier smiled at her. "How are you?"

"Fit but a little tired. George still wakes in the night to be fed."

The older man's smile stretched wide as his gaze moved to the baby seat. "My first grandson." He strode around the table. "Last time I saw you, you were a bump in your mummy's tummy."

Everyone laughed.

"George junior. Good choice of name!" Brigadier Knight gripped George's foot and shook it. "He's a handsome chap. He's obviously taken after his grandfather."

The mood in the room bubbled with joy and merriment as everyone laughed again. Olivia watched the brigadier meet his grandson, yet most of her attention focused on Radley. His gaze settled on George, then moved back to her. She returned his appraisal. Longing pulsed through her as their eyes met.

She had started to wonder if she really loved him as much as she thought. The yearning inside her confirmed she did. Her heart wanted to burst out of her chest with pleasure at seeing him again. She couldn't wait to be alone with him, to feel his arms around her. From the expression on his face, he felt the same way.

"Well," said Brigadier Knight, breaking into her warm imaginings of being with Radley. She swung her gaze towards the older man. He gave her a considered look, then moved on to appraise Cameron. "When are you going to make an honest woman of Olivia and ask her to marry you?"

Olivia froze, hardly able to believe the brigadier had said such a thing. Cameron's face paled but she gave him only a passing glance, her attention jumping to Radley. His lazy smile faded to a fixed blank expression.

"I hardly think that's our business," Sandra said, breaking the awkward silence.

"Of course it is." Brigadier Knight gripped the back of a chair. "My grandson will grow up in a proper family with a mother and father. I did not raise my sons to shirk their responsibilities, did I?" He turned his stern gaze on Cameron and raised questioning eyebrows.

Radley had been about to walk around the table to take his turn greeting Olivia and George. His thoughts had drifted back to the nights he'd spent in her room before he left, the simple pleasure of holding her in his arms while she slept and the other pleasures he now hoped they could enjoy together.

His father's words slashed across his senses, waking him from his fantasy with a painful jolt. For a moment his mind blanked in shock, then he took in Olivia's stricken expression and Cameron's obvious embarrassment.

This was awkward beyond words. If only he had confided in his father how he felt about Olivia. He had never liked to discuss personal matters with his parents, but maybe he should have made an exception this time. He'd had plenty of opportunity during the journey home.

Radley gripped the back of his neck, trying to decide what to do. Tension vibrated through the family gathering. Now was not the moment to confess his feelings and possibly embarrass Olivia further. He needed to speak to both her and Cameron in private first.

Radley met Olivia's desperate gaze and longed to wrap her in his arms and tell her not to worry. Instead he satisfied himself with a quick kiss on her cheek. "Talk upstairs in a minute," he whispered before he withdrew.

His mother chatted, trying to smooth things over. His father looked on with the demeanor of a man who expected everyone to jump to it and do as they were told.

"I think I'll take my stuff upstairs," Radley said, giving his mother's shoulder a reassuring squeeze. "Is Cam sleeping in my room with me?"

"Yes, darling." Clutching at the lifeline of normality Radley had thrown, his mother rose and hurried in front of him to the hall cupboard. "Cameron, you can use the camp bed."

For once Cameron didn't complain. He simply hoisted the folded bed and carted it up the stairs. Radley passed his mother the sack of Christmas presents he'd bought in London and followed his brother, moving ahead on the landing to open the bedroom door.

Once in the sanctuary of his room, Radley dumped his bag on the floor and went to stare out the window. It was dark outside. Two lamps spilled pools of light, one on the terrace and the other beside the pond, highlighting the glistening cobweb of ice across the water and the sparkling frost-encrusted tree branches. A few fluffy snowflakes spiraled out of the sky and settled on the ground.

Radley rested a hand on the window frame and pulled his thoughts together. He and his brother didn't generally discuss their feelings, but he needed to ask

Cameron a question. He was almost certain he knew the answer, yet he had to be sure before he said anything else. Radley glanced over his shoulder.

Cameron had spread out on Radley's bed and was checking his phone.

"Do you love Olivia?" Radley said.

Cameron's gaze jumped to him, startled. "What? No. I don't. And I'm not going to marry her, so don't you start pressuring me as well. This is the twenty-first century. Women can have babies without being married."

Relief burned through Radley, leaving a pleasant afterglow like a gulp of double malt. "Don't worry. We'll sort it out."

"Yeah. By telling Dad to stop living in the past."

Radley couldn't help smiling. "Good luck with that."

Cameron scowled.

Radley dropped down on the edge of the bed and wondered how attached Cameron had become to George. That would be the complication. "There's an easy way to get Dad off your back. I'll marry Olivia."

"You?" Cameron's brows knitted. "You don't even know her. Why would you—"

"I *do* know her. I was here for the first six weeks of George's life."

"You've known her for six weeks and you want to marry her?"

"We were together 24/7."

"Really?" Cameron sat up and eyed him curiously. "At night as well?"

"I love her, Cam. That's all you need to know."

Cameron chewed the corner of his lip. "That means you'll become George's stepfather."

"I won't cut you out, Cam. You can see George whenever you want. You'll still be an important part of his life."

Cameron flopped back on the pillow and threw an

arm over his face. For long minutes he was silent. Nerves churned in Radley's gut. He didn't want to steal his brother's son, but Olivia and George were a package. He loved them both. Cameron did not.

"Look, she'll end up marrying someone. If it's me, then you're far more likely to see George regularly."

Cameron blew out a breath and uncovered his face. "I kinda thought Olivia would be too busy to have a boyfriend. I guess that was stupid."

And selfish, Radley thought. But he kept that to himself. No point in stirring things up. His gaze moved to the wall, knowing that on the other side was the room where Olivia and George slept, the room where he so badly wanted to be right now. "I already love that little boy as if he were my own," he said softly. "I will love them both and look after them."

Cameron's eyes watered and Radley felt bad. Perhaps he should have taken this more slowly or approached it differently. He rested a hand on his brother's shoulder. "I'm sorry, Cam. But you've got to think of what's best for Olivia as well."

"Yeah, I know." He rubbed his eyes with the heels of his hands. "I just wanted to be George's dad."

"You can see him every time you have leave. If that's what you want."

Cameron leaned back against the headboard and fiddled with his phone. "Have you asked her if she'll marry you?"

"No."

"You sure she'll say yes?"

Radley shrugged, not wanting to delve into his own fears and insecurities.

"You better go and do the deed." Cameron punched him on the arm halfheartedly. "Good luck."

"Yeah, thanks."

Radley's heart thumped as he left his room and knocked softly on the one next door. When Olivia answered, he slipped inside.

She had obviously just changed George's diaper and placed him on the bed so she could put on her nightdress and feed him. A tentative smile lit her face at the sight of Radley.

"I'm sorry, Liv, I wanted to greet you properly, but it was awkward downstairs. I've missed you so much." He went to her and she stepped into his arms. For a few moments he simply held her, his cheek against her hair, reveling in the feel of her slender body against him. Then he dipped his head. She met his lips in a welcoming kiss that seared away his fear that she might not care for him as he hoped.

After long moments, they broke apart when George whimpered as if demanding his turn to say hello.

Radley picked up the baby and held him close, pressing his lips to the soft, dark hair. "You are growing into such a big boy. Mummy must be looking after you well." Radley rocked him to and fro, a stupid grin on his face.

Olivia leaned in and rested her head on his shoulder. He shifted George into one arm so he could wrap his other around her.

"He's able to hold his head up quite well now," she said. "It won't be long before he can sit up. I can't wait for him to be able to sit in a high chair at the table."

"Then he'll be crawling and walking." Radley's thoughts rolled on through the months, imagining the three of them together as George grew into a little boy. Radley would teach him to ride a bike and kick a ball. And he'd make sure to include Cameron so he didn't miss anything.

George nuzzled the front of Radley's shirt and Olivia giggled.

"You're not going to get any grub from me, you little scamp. You need Mummy for that."

Radley handed the baby back to Olivia, impressed by

how much heavier he had grown in the last month. She laid George on her bed and picked up her nightie. "I was just going to change." Her cheeks flushed.

"I need to put on my pajamas and brush my teeth," Radley said, realizing she wanted a few minutes of privacy. "Can I come back?"

Radley had made the mistake of distancing himself from Olivia before he left for Wales. He wasted precious nights when he could have been with her. He told himself he was doing the right thing, giving her space to decide how she felt about Cameron ahead of his visit. What he really did was allow his horrible experience with his ex-wife to influence his actions.

That was in the past and had no bearing on this situation. He didn't want to be alone any more. He wanted to spend every moment he could with Olivia and George.

"Yes, come back." Olivia gripped his hand. He kissed her again, relief flashing through him. This Christmas was the start of the rest of his life. He had a second chance. He'd get it right this time.

Chapter Nine

Olivia's breath rushed out on a little gasp of relief and pleasure. When Radley's arms closed around her, the recent weeks of uncertainty melted away like a distant memory. It was as if he hadn't been away. She loved this man so much. She never wanted to let him go again.

When he went to change, she did a circuit of the room, switched on the Christmas lights strung along the wall beside George's crib, and lit the scented candles on top of the chest of drawers and bedside tables. Then she turned off the main light. A soft glow fell over the bed and a festive, spicy fragrance filled the room. She had hoped and prayed things might work out this way, but hardly dared believe that as the clock struck twelve to herald Christmas Day, she would be snuggled in bed with Radley.

She dug out the blue silk negligee she rarely wore, quickly changed, and dashed to the bathroom where she freshened up, and applied a few strategic dabs of perfume. Then she climbed in bed, leaned against a stack of pillows, and fed George.

Fifteen minutes later, Radley slipped back in the door, a robe over his pajamas. He paused and glanced around, a smile lifting the corners of his mouth. "It's so good to be here with you again."

He rounded the bed and sniffed the air near the scented candle. "Smells nice," he said, shrugging off his robe. He tossed it onto a chair, then lifted the covers to climb in beside her.

Nerves tingled beneath her skin. They had done nothing more than kiss before he left. She had still been recovering from her C-section and Radley had been very gentle with her. Now she was fully fit, there was no reason why they couldn't make love.

Radley lay on his side watching her, his head propped up on his hand. When George had finished, she kissed her little boy good night and, just as he'd done many times before, Radley took him and settled him in his crib.

He climbed in beside her again and they lay facing each other, his large, warm hand clasping hers on the pillow between them. "I'm sorry, Olivia, sorry I distanced myself from you before I left, and sorry I shipped out without coming home to say good-bye properly."

He pressed his lips to the back of her hand, eyes closed. "I've been waiting weeks to talk to you. I needed to discuss things face-to-face, e-mail and text were too impersonal."

"I understand." She stroked her palm over his stubbly jaw, the roughness giving her a little zing of pleasure.

"I'm guessing you don't want to marry Cameron."

Olivia gave a startled laugh. "No!"

"That's good." Radley grinned, then leaned closer and kissed her. "Now I can move on to the important part."

He pulled a small red box out from under his pillow and set it on the sheet between them. Olivia's breath hitched. A light-headed sense of anticipation filled her.

Lifting the lid, he revealed a beautiful marquise-cut diamond ring. "Will you marry me, Olivia?" Radley whispered.

She pressed her hand to her heart, overwhelmed with surprise and pleasure. She loved him and knew he loved her, but had never dreamed he'd propose so soon. "Are you sure?"

He laughed. "You were on my mind the whole time I was away. I'm sure."

"Yes, Radley. Yes, I'd love to."

He slipped the ring on her finger. She kissed him and snuggled in his arms, staring at her hand with a sense of wonder and unreality. She felt as though she were floating in a dream—she, George, and Radley would be a proper family.

The grandfather clock on the landing chimed the hour. They listened together in the warm cocoon of their bed as midnight sounded. "Merry Christmas," Radley said, pressing a kiss to her lips. "Let's make our announcement at dinner tomorrow."

"That should make your father happy."

"It'll make me happy." Radley pulled her closer and slid a gentle hand down her back, trailing a row of kisses from beneath her ear to her collarbone. "Now, my darling fiancée, there's something else I've been dreaming about while I've been away."

"It must be the same thing I've been dreaming about." Olivia giggled as his tiny ticklish kisses moved lower.

"The perfect way to welcome in Christmas Day," Radley whispered.

Radley woke and pushed up on an elbow. He smiled down at Olivia, still fast asleep, her dark hair spread across the pillow in a silky fan. He pressed a soft kiss to her temple before he slid out of bed.

Happy gurgling sounds came from George's crib. The baby had kicked off his covers and was trying to roll over. His chubby face beamed a grin when Radley leaned over the wooden bars. "You're a happy little guy, aren't you?"

George had woken for a feed at six a.m. He could wait a while longer for his next one. Radley had kept Olivia up late, so he wanted to give her a chance to sleep in.

He picked the baby up, changed his diaper, and slipped out of the bedroom, shutting the door quietly. When Radley entered his own room, Cameron was dead to the world, sprawled across the bed where Radley had left him last night.

He laid George on the covers for a moment. The baby wriggled, making happy sounds, while Radley pulled on jeans and a T-shirt. Then he gathered the little lad into his arms and took him downstairs.

The familiar smell of roasting turkey carried Radley back through the years to many other happy family Christmases with his parents. He wanted this day to be perfect for Olivia and George. Olivia hadn't enjoyed the same close family he had. From now on he would make sure she did.

Wandering through the house, he showed George the sparkling Christmas decorations. The baby boy's eyes fixed on the flashing lights on the decorated tree in the sitting room. Radley went down on a knee to show George the heap of brightly wrapped presents, and noticed his mother had added the gifts he'd brought.

The baby stretched out a hand. Radley smiled. "Not yet, Georgie Porgie. You get to unwrap your presents after lunch." He put his mouth to the baby's ear and whispered, "But I can let you in on a secret, the ones in blue paper are from me." He'd gone a little overboard and bought far too many toys. He and his father had made a special trip to the huge Hamleys toy store on Regent Street before they left London.

Radley toured the room, pointing out the garland of glossy green holly with scarlet berries draped over the roaring log fire, the fat Santa on the windowsill, which they'd owned since Radley was a boy, and the glittering baubles on the Christmas tree.

They wandered into the dining room. The festive red tablecloth already covered the table, and another log fire burned in the grate.

The sound of his parents' voices drew Radley to the kitchen. His father sat at the table reading the newspaper while his mother peeled potatoes. "Merry Christmas." Radley kissed his mother's cheek. "I'll give you a hand with that, if you like."

"No, you won't. You take it easy." She turned a delighted grin on him. "From what your father says, you've had a busy few days in the halls of power at the MOD with your clever father. I can't wait to tell everyone he's now a major general." Her face glowed with pride.

His father peered over his newspaper. "Don't tell anyone yet. It's not official until the New Year."

Radley smiled to himself at his mother's excitement. He hoped his family would be as thrilled by the announcement he and Olivia planned to make over Christmas dinner.

Olivia sat at the desk with a shaving mirror angled towards the light and applied her makeup. George squealed with laughter behind her. She glanced over her shoulder, her pulse picking up pace at the sight of Radley relaxed on the bed in his faded jeans and a blue shirt. He was leaning over, blowing on George's tummy, making him kick and wriggle with delight.

They were both engrossed in the game. "You like that, Georgie Porgie, don't you?" Radley said.

Happiness bubbled inside Olivia. Radley was so kind and thoughtful. He'd let her sleep in, and she'd certainly needed it after last night. His gaze rose to her as if sensing her appraisal. The corners of his lips kicked into a crooked smile. Pleasure zinged along her nerves at memories of being in his arms.

"You look even more beautiful than usual this morning," he said. "That red dress is stunning, although I preferred what you were wearing before you put it on."

She giggled and tossed one of George's soft toys at him. Grinning, he caught it.

"I don't think your parents would approve if I went down for Christmas dinner in black lacy underwear."

"I'd approve, though."

For long moments, they stared into each other's eyes, a hot pulse of anticipation passing between them. She would enjoy Christmas Day with the Knights, but she was looking forward to later when she and Radley could be alone again.

George squealed and the moment passed.

Olivia returned to her makeup, keeping half an eye on Radley's reflection in the mirror. She loved him so much. Since he came home, her life had been like a dream; he'd declared his love and asked her to marry him. She wanted to exist in this fantasy bubble of happiness forever, but her practical worries nipped at her thoughts.

"Will you be able to take the rest of your leave now?"

"Most of it. I want to talk to you about that. I have four weeks off, then I'm going to Oxfordshire."

"Oxfordshire?" Olivia swiveled around on the stool to see him better. "As in the other side of London?"

Radley laughed. "That's where it was the last time I looked at a map."

She knew Radley was committed to his job. If she wanted to marry him, she must accept that. Lying in his arms after they had made love last night, she had decided she would always support him, even if it meant she had to cope alone while he was on a tour of duty in some far-flung part of the world. But she would much rather have him safely in the UK, even if they weren't always together.

"How long before you're sent abroad again?"

Although she tried to keep her voice casual, Radley must have picked up the concern in her tone. He climbed off the bed and came to her. "Don't worry, love. I won't be sent away for a while. Oxfordshire is my new posting, and it sounds like something long-term, although one can never be sure." He crouched beside her and took her hands, his thumb caressing her finger beside the engagement ring.

"There's a new military hospital being built near RAF Brize Norton. It's still under construction, but it will be a fantastic facility when it's finished. State of the art. Currently they're using part of it as a clearing station for seriously wounded forces personnel who are flown back to the UK. I'm going to head up the orthopedic unit there. It'll give me a chance to do more research into my specialty. I've been swapping ideas with Sean Fabian, a plastic surgeon. We're working on protocols for dealing with battlefield trauma."

Olivia's eyes widened, and her heart thumped with relief. She had been steeling herself to cope with his absence, worrying he would be sent somewhere dangerous. The enthusiasm in his voice as he spoke of the new appointment made her realize this was something special, something very important to him. "It sounds like congratulations are in order."

"I would say so. The senior officer who told me indicated I could expect a promotion in a few months. That means a pay raise."

"That's wonderful. Well done." She wrapped her arms around his neck and kissed him. "Will I be able to see you regularly?"

"You'll be able to see me every day. We'll move into army married quarters to start with, then when we're settled in the area, we'll look for a place to buy." He laughed. "I was disappointed when you texted me about losing Brook View Cottage, but it's turned out to be a blessing in disguise."

Married so quickly. After the uncertain weeks of waiting, things now seemed to be happening fast. Olivia clung to Radley, feeling a little light-headed. "Do you have a date in mind?"

"As soon as possible. The army won't give us married quarters unless we're married. I want to be with you, love." He curved his palm around her cheek. "That's what you want, isn't it?"

"Yes, oh yes." Olivia buried her face in Radley's neck. She'd felt so totally alone and frightened in the hospital waiting to give birth. She'd lost her apartment because she couldn't work to pay the rent, and had nobody to turn to for help. First Sandra, then Radley had been generous and kind. They'd given her hope that things would work out—and they had. "Thank you, Radley. Thank you so much for being there for me, for giving me this chance at happiness."

Radley laughed wryly. "I'm the one who should be thanking you, sweetheart." He pulled back and stroked the hair off her face. "I was living a half life, focused completely on my job with zero personal life. I thought I'd handled what happened with my ex-wife, but meeting you and George made me realize I was still letting her mess with my head. You and George were a wake-up call. There is a whole lot more to life, and I was missing out."

Radley leaned his forehead against hers. "You're everything I want. I'm lucky I found you."

"You're my knight in shining armor, Radley. I love you so much. To think that when I first discovered I was pregnant, I thought my life was ruined. It's turned out to be the best thing that ever happened to me. If it wasn't for George, I wouldn't have met you."

***

Christmas dinner was a cheerful affair with the men chatting about their work and George gurgling happily, chewing on a teething toy and covering his cute Santa bib with drool. When the turkey had been eaten, Radley pulled the diamond engagement ring out of his pocket, where he'd hidden it until their official announcement, and cast Olivia a glance full of suppressed excitement.

"We have something to tell you," he said.

Sandra paused as she gathered the dirty dishes, and Brigadier Knight pinned his eldest son with a curious look.

Radley pushed the ring onto Olivia's finger and Sandra gasped. "I asked Olivia to marry me, and she said yes!" He kissed her and they both grinned.

"Oh, this is wonderful." Sandra jumped up and rushed around the table, hugging first Radley, then Olivia. "I'm so pleased for you both, and little Georgie."

Brigadier Knight's gaze traveled between Radley and Cameron. "This isn't how I expected things to work out, but it will do." He smiled and nodded. "Congratulations." He rose and shook Radley's hand, then slapped him on the back. "Second time lucky, hey."

Sandra rolled her eyes. "Men," she said under her breath to Olivia. "They never quite say the right thing, do they?" But Olivia was too happy to worry and from the grin on Radley's face, his first marriage was far from his mind.

Cameron was slower to congratulate them. He stood and moved to George, gazing thoughtfully at the baby before coming around the table and embracing Olivia. "Congratulations. I hope you'll be happy."

Radley turned to him. There was a moment of awkwardness as they stared at each other before they hugged. "You're okay with this?" Radley asked.

"Yeah, of course. Well done, mate."

"Champagne," Sandra called over the hubbub, before disappearing out the door. She came back with a bottle and a corkscrew, struggled with it for a second or two, then handed it to her husband. In a few minutes they all had fizzing flutes of Dom Pérignon.

Radley curled his arm around Olivia's shoulders and happiness zinged through her. She hadn't just found a wonderful man to spend her life with, she had found a family, a wonderful family who had welcomed her and her son.

"To Radley and Olivia," Brigadier Knight said. "May they have many happy years together."

"And to baby George," Sandra added. "May Radley and Olivia give him lots of brothers and sisters."

"Hear, hear," Brigadier Knight said.

Radley waggled his eyebrows, making Olivia giggle as she raised her glass to tap it against his.

"To happy families," she said, knowing how lucky she was to have found her happy family and for them all to be together at Christmas.

The Army Doctor's Wedding

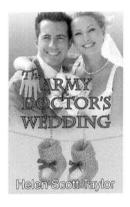

Major Cameron Knight thrives on the danger of front-line battlefield medicine. Throwing himself into saving the lives of injured servicemen keeps the demons from his past away. When he rescues charity worker, Alice Conway, and a tiny newborn baby, he longs for a second chance to do the right thing, even if it means marrying a woman he barely knows so they can take the orphan baby to England for surgery. The brave, beautiful young woman and the orphan baby steal his heart. He wants to make the marriage real, but being married to an army officer who's stationed overseas might do her more harm than good.

Praise for The Army Doctor's Wedding

"Grab a Kleenex because you are going to need it! This is one no romance lover should miss!" Teresa Hughes

"The book starts out with lots of action and holds the reader's interest through to the end. It's a great read!" Sue E. Pennington

The Army Doctor's Christmas Baby

After he loses his wife, army surgeon Colonel Sean Fabian protects his damaged heart by cutting women out of his life. He dedicates himself to his career and being a great dad to his twin babies. When he asks army nurse Kelly Grace to play nanny to his children over Christmas, he realizes how much he misses having a beautiful woman in his life and in his arms. Caring for Sean's adorable twin babies is Kelly's dream come true. She falls in love with the sweet little girls and their daddy, but she's hiding a devastating event from the past. If she can't trust Sean with her secret, how can she ever expect him to trust her with his bruised heart?

Praise for The Army Doctor's Christmas Baby

"...if you want to experience the true essence of Christmas, with the love and understanding that only being with family over the holidays can satisfy, you'll definitely want to experience, The Army Doctor's Christmas Baby." F Barnett

About the Author

Helen Scott Taylor won the American Title IV contest in 2008. Her winning book, The Magic Knot, was published in 2009 to critical acclaim, received a starred review from *Booklist*, and was a *Booklist* top ten romance for 2009. Since then, she has published other novels, novellas, and short stories in both the UK and USA.

Helen lives in South West England near Plymouth in Devon between the windswept expanse of Dartmoor and the rocky Atlantic coast. As well as her wonderful long-suffering husband, she shares her home with a Westie a Shih Tzu and an aristocratic chocolate-shaded-silver-burmilla cat who rules the household with a velvet paw. She believes that deep within everyone, there's a little magic.

Find Helen at:

http://www.HelenScottTaylor.com
http://twitter.com/helenscotttaylo
http://facebook.com/helenscotttaylor
www.facebook.com/HelenScottTaylorAuthor

Book List

Paranormal/Fantasy Romance

The Magic Knot
The Phoenix Charm
The Ruby Kiss
The Feast of Beauty
Warriors of Ra
A Clockwork Fairytale
Ice Gods
Cursed Kiss

Contemporary Romance

The Army Doctor's Wedding
The Army Doctor's Christmas Baby
Unbreak My Heart
Oceans Between Us
Finally Home
A Family for Christmas
A Family Forever
Moments of Gold
Flowers on the water

Young Adult

Wildwood

Printed in Great Britain
by Amazon